Mars Life

by Kevin Shoemaker

Shoemakerlabs, Publishers

This is a work of fiction. All the characters and events portrayed in this novel are either fictitious or are used fictitiously.

MARS LIFE

This book is printed on acid free paper

A Shoemaker Labs Book
Lafayette, Colorado
www.shoemakerlabs.com

ISBN 978-0-9815092-1-1
ISBN 0-9815092-1-5

Cover Art courtesy of NASA
Chapter Artwork courtesy of MarsSociety.org

First edition February, 2008

Printed in the United States of America

To Judi, Leah and Stephen
for their inspiration and support

Acknowledgment

I would like to sincerely thank the Mars Society in general and Dr. Robert Zubrin in particular for their generosity and comments. Also, I would like to thank my friends Matt, Jason, and Eliot for their editing and comments. My father deserves credit in being the 1st person to read this and pronounce it worthy, thank you. Finally, I would like to thank my lovely wife Judi for her editing and encouragement.

Author's Note

This is a book of Science Fiction in the strictest sense, not Science Fantasy. Some of what you will read actually happened as I had the great luck of spending two weeks at the Mars Society's Mars Desert Research Station in Utah in 2003. The experience there was the catalyst for this book.

Many of the ideas contained herein are feasible and in the hands of competent scientists and engineers, achievable. It was the intent while writing this book to piece together several promising technologies, assume the kinks had been worked out and present them in such a way as to allow more informed readers to believe that the dots, if connected, could indeed allow the story to be one of history as apposed to one of fiction.

The single motivating force behind this book is the energy collected by the author, over the years, from a multitude of very competent individuals, who in concert could actually make a difference in our civilization. These people are from all walks of life and over the last several years have turned into great scientists, engineers and teachers. By shear luck, they have crossed paths with me and allowed me to realize that the focusing of such quality intellect would allow us as a civilization in general to move up a notch and solve some difficult problems, none the least of which is the trip to Mars and back. Today most people do not think of this adventure as impossible, just expensive. And, expense is relative. It is relative to how much we spend on other facets of our society. This of course is based on how people in general perceive risk, threats, and the usefulness of more ambitious goals. Our priorities constantly move and morph to accommodate a new crisis, and it seems that this kind of lifestyle is more reactive than proactive. Generally, I believe, the vast majority of people do not wish for war, famine or lack of education, but that is what we have. In this reality, we tend to push more positive values aside to address a more present dangers or concerns allowing the darker activities to take place.

Can we move forward? Of course, in fact we must, if we are interested in survival as a people. It is in our nature to explore, question and grow.

This book opens a conceptual door to the path of moving forward so please read it with an open mind. Be more critical in examining the ideas as potentially feasible, and for a bit, place yourselves in the position of a casual observer.

K. Shoemaker
Washington, D.C. 2007

Part 1 of Mars Life

Chapter 1:   The crew

"What a ride"

Stephen Daedalus dusted the red dirt off of his boots and wondered what on earth he was doing here. This was a strange question coming from a person who was just starting a scientific simulation of life on Mars as he stopped for a moment to stare at his boots and time travel to the future when someone would be doing the same thing on the Red Planet. A long drive of seven hours through the mountains of Colorado into the canyon lands of Southern Utah left him tired and hungry. At the last turn through the off world looking Mesozoic landscape, he saw the hab. It stood about 30 feet tall and was 30 feet in diameter with a red, green and blue flag flying nearby. The hab was white with decals of sponsors displayed and from within came a humming sound. Stephen stopped and listened, the sound reminded him of a ship or jetliner and he thought, "this place is alive". A drum shaped green hab was situated to the East of the main building with bubbling tanks of hydroponic fluid filtering effluent and providing water for several barrels of water lilies.

"This should be interesting," he thought.

He was concerned that for several weeks he would be cooped up with a bunch of sci-fi nerds or worse, a bunch of dreamers whose lights were on but nobody home. He shut the van door, took a small suitcase and headed to the "door"; which was really a mock airlock complete with a circular port hole window and crank style door handles. The hinges ran the length of the right side and looked comparable with an airliner style door. It was heavy but before Stephen pulled it open he heard laughter inside and with a anxious complexion thought, "Oh boy, here we go." The door was opened and inside he found an airlock simulator complete with lights and pressure gages. The airlock was cylindrical, six feet wide, painted white with two doors. The second door inside allowed him into the EVA room which housed six spacesuits, six Plexiglas helmets and six air circulating back packs. Also, in this area were boxes of gloves, racks of boots and a line of radios that hung on the far wall.

"Well they have paid attention to detail." Further inside was a decent laboratory, mostly for geological and biological work. Plenty of space was available for other experiments though. There were microscopes, test tubes and various chemicals on the tables. All walls were curved and as a consequence, so were all lab benches and cabinets. To the right was a set of stairs that ascended 10 feet at a steep incline.

"The only way up is sideways," thought Stephen.

He put the suitcase down knowing that it would be a challenge to take anything up or down these stairs, which looked like they had been designed for use in a submarine. Voices upstairs drew him up and going sideways and holding onto a rail, he ascended sometimes hitting a knee on the wooden structure or rail. Above in the living quarters were several people, one of whom he recognized. This was Benny Radachi, a PhD chemist who Stephen had met at the Mars Society conventions and again at an astronautics company run by Dr. Zubrin, who had build the hab.

"Hey, you made it," said Benny, "How was the drive?".

"Ok," lamented Stephen, "Pretty slow in the ski traffic, but after that uneventful. This is an amazing place, situated out here in the middle of no where, Utah. Great geology and a beautiful sky."

"Yep," said Benny, "Its going to be rejuvenating as well. By the way I want to introduce you to some of our crew, crew 12. The previous crew, crew 11 is outside going for a walk, so we have a few moments to get to know one another."

Pointing to his left, Benny said, "This is Sally, from the U.K. and Ingmar from the Netherlands."

"Hello," said Sally, "And you are?"

"Stephen, Stephen Daedalus from Colorado, how are you?" "Great," said Sally. Stephen shook her hand and shook Ingmar's as well.

"Nice to meet you, Stephen," said Ingmar. "Where is Colorado?"

"The next state to the East, I am from Boulder, near Denver," said Stephen.

After the pleasantries, Stephen looked around to find six small staterooms in an arc taking up about 1/3 of the upper deck. The rest of the area was made up of a kitchen and curved tables for the laptop computers that everyone would bring. Finally, at the end of the curved space there was a TV monitor and another laptop computer for working the remote observatories outside. One of the observatories was a radio telescope designed to observe the radio emission of Jupiter and also of the Sun. The other, optical observatory held an 11 inch "go-to" telescope with a fine CCD camera and filter wheel attached. In the center of the living space was a rectangular table, looking a bit strange in an all curved environment. However this would be the meeting and eating place for the next several weeks. Stephen opened up a stateroom for a peek.

"You can have that one if you want," said Benny. Inside the stateroom was a bed made like a large bookshelf, cantilevered out of the wall. The platform was about five feet above the floor. Below that was the wall of the next stateroom, whose bed would be closer to the floor. An efficient use of space. At the end of the stateroom was a shelf for personal items and hooks for various things. All rooms were equipped with Ethernet cables, which connected to a satellite dish network place on the roof of the hab. This network also had cables in the main living area around the curved work table up against the wall. Four or five laptops would reside there for this rotation, for writing e-mails and reports. These laptops would emulate the computer nerve center required on a real voyage to Mars.

For the first time, Stephen felt an inkling of actually being in the craft that would be on it's way to the Red Planet. He had applied for a job with Zubrin's company as an engineer.   He ended up as a consultant and worked on several projects that were designed to understand certain properties of the planet. Mars has a very thin atmosphere, about the same as the earth's at an altitude of 90,000 feet. The temperature at that altitude was also about the same as Mars'. To inflate balloons or other structures, experiments had to be done at that altitude. Stephen's duties included designing computer systems and deployment methods that would work at that altitude, temperature (as it is very cold up there) and ultimately in a carbon dioxide environment. Stephen had become friends with Zubrin and the other engineers and workers at the astronautics company and came to realize that these people took the voyage to Mars seriously.   Money was available from several scientific organizations, notably NASA, to do this kind of research. As a result of the work and inspiration from the Mars activities, Stephen had been asked to participate in a rotation of crew members studying procedures for the eventual trip to Mars. He had accepted and within several weeks, found himself standing in this Mars simulation habitat in the middle of Utah.

Mars Life

What would the people be like he wondered, given the fact that they would be coming from all over the globe, without any prior meetings (with the exception of Stephen and Benny). This would indeed be interesting and as far as Benny was concerned, Stephen had not worked closely with him, nor did he know Benny's personality very well. Benny appeared quiet and spent most of his time in an office doing chemical equations and other similar endeavors while Stephen dropped by periodically to work with other members of the astronautics company.

Well, now is the time to find out some things, thought Stephen. "So Benny, where is the rest of the crew?" he asked.

"On their way and should be here soon," answered Benny. "As far as crew 11 is concerned, they will be here tonight along with us, and then will return to Salt Lake City tomorrow in the 'un-pressurized rover'."

As it turns out, the un-pressurized rover was an old Air Force four wheel drive truck sitting outside by Stephen's van. Not exactly a smooth ride for the tired crew. Considering that Stephen brought a conversion van, and this would be an opportunity to learn about how these rotations were conducted, he thought that it could be advantageous to drive the other crew back.

"If you would like Benny, I could take them back

tomorrow morning, it might be a bit more comfortable," asked Stephen.

Benny thought for a moment and said, "If it is not too much trouble, that would be great."

"Power bars, bring back power bars," said Sally, "We are going to be doing a lot of hiking."

Crew 11 came back from their trek, walking lethargically. They appeared tired, hungry, yet very happy. Tomorrow he would find out much more about them on the way to the Salt Lake Airport.

The rest of the new crew showed up by dusk. While they unpacked and moved inside the hab, they paused to see that the sunset was extraordinary, giving the image of a tranquil Mars outpost during the changing of the crews. On Mars this will mean a crew rotation period of between one and two years with a voyage of six to 36 weeks, each way will be necessary. The difference in time will be based on the kinds of rocket propulsion available then. Stephen had that feeling again of how it really will be on that outpost some day. It was much like deja-vu only about the future, not the past.

He started to unload his van in anticipation of the ride the next day. Not knowing how much to bring, Stephen decided to bring "it all." Insofar as he wanted to simulate finding water underneath the Martian surface, he brought a remote control aircraft and a robotic ground rover. The ground rover was borrowed from Acroname, a company that specialized in intelligent robotic systems. Stephen had met the principles and worked with them toward a viable ground penetrating radar platform. This ground penetrating radar was one of the best tools to examine subterranean features, including water. It is assumed and hoped that there is a lot of water underneath the Martian soil. Spacecraft orbiting Mars have detected the molecules that indicate the presence of water. Also, an analysis of photographs have shown a lot of water erosion artifacts in the Martian landscape. Obviously, any water found in the Martian soil will allow life to propagate (maybe once again) above or below the surface. Stephen knew the major importance of developing equipment and procedures for this research, as it surely would be part of the first voyage, if not on preceding robotic explorations.

Stephen also brought other electronic equipment including an air deployable meteorological station with a navigation beacon. This "met" station would serve several purposes on Mars. Many would be "sprinkled" around the surface and particularly near the landing zone. First the stations would be used as navigation beacons for EVA teams and airborne vehicles. Secondly as a part of a meteorological "web" to best measure and understand

Martian weather. Before any EVAs, the weather must be known to prevent astronauts and cosmonauts from being caught in a dust storm or other potentially hazardous weather. Third, the stations could be used for emergency communications in the event of a suit radio failure.

Finally, he had brought a medium power amateur radio station. This included the long distance short wave transceiver as well as higher frequency equipment that would allow members of crew 12 to communicate with astronauts and cosmonauts in the space station and space shuttle that were going to be flying overhead during the next several weeks. Mars he knew, had an ionosphere and could be used for long distance short wave communications using similar equipment. The challenge would be to find the optimum frequency for the time of day (which would vary) and to be able to deal with the interference caused by the Sun and Jupiter. Large antennas for use in this kind of communications could be easily erected on Mars, thought Stephen, due to fact that it has .38 times the gravity of earth. In fact, this low gravity would have several beneficial effects, none the least of which would be the simple construction techniques needed to house the crews.

Boxes, books and equipment were eventually brought out of the van and placed in the laboratory section of the hab. It had turned into night time, Stephen decided to go up and talk some more to the new and old inhabitants. Before he went up, he stopped before entering and felt a bit alone. He was isolated from friends and family. These new people were now "the new world" and starting from ground level made him feel a bit apprehensive. These feelings would last no more that 24 hours when he would find out that the new crew was made up of extraordinary like minded people with enough drive and intellectual capability to solve big problems. Stephen's life was about to change.

Upstairs, he found the two crews exchanging information regarding the daily operations of the hab. The commander demonstrated the donning of the space suits, transfer of water, use of the toilet facilities (which employed an incinolet) and green hab operations.

The whole idea of the Mars Analog Station is to simulate the daily ritual of living on the Red Planet. This will consist of conserving water (until more is found), using waste water to feed plants that produce food and oxygen, using minimal energy for light and other living functions by employing solar cells, batteries and minimal chemical fuel usage. As the experience on Mars grows, the new inhabitants will find sources for energy, materials for building and will be able to break down the CO_2 atmosphere to provide oxygen for breathing. It is interesting, Stephen mused, how none of the other planets or moons provide the building blocks for habitation as Mars does. It is also interesting to realize that Mars has the surface area equivalent to all of the continents of earth combined. Another earth but without the oceans, he thought. It is time for the exploration to begin and the first personal experience can be had at this hab. This is the tabula rasa for the future.

The crews continued to talk, and Stephen noticed a large vertical line drawn on a white board in the living area. This was labeled "stress level" and started at zero near the bottom and topped off at "getting violent." Stephen realized that there had been some sociological problems due to poorly acting equipment or facilities in the hab due to the fact that and indicator arrow had been drawn at various places along the line, sometimes coming close to the top. Looking around and listening, Stephen discovered that the plumbing sometimes worked and had recently completely backed up, leaving a very vile smell emanating in the hab. Also, the gas and water could be mis-used to the point of extinction. The gas was used to run a generator about 100 meters from the hab, providing electricity. It also provided the hum Stephen noticed upon arrival. There was a finite supply of both and to run out either was to cause an emergency. Clearly, someone like an engineer had to be responsible for the facilities and manage the resources of the hab. The engineer position would be challenging and require a sense of responsibility toward the well being of the rest of the crew. On the real voyage, this engineer would perform a very similar task that would ultimately allow the other crew members to concentrate on their respective duties.

The old crew seemed happy, sad and tired. As it was getting late in the evening, everyone needed rest and soon the lights were dimmed, sleeping bags came out and minutes later, all were asleep.

The next morning, confusion set in briefly with the old crew moving out, new crew moving in, everyone trying to eat breakfast and the two commanders exchanging the baton. Benny was the new commander, he was by far the most experienced in the operations of the habitat as he had been on previous crews and would be able to set the tone necessary for everyone to have a great experience.

As the dust settled and the old crew gathered around the van for departure, the new crew member could finally meet each other and talk a bit. Vasili was a PhD student from California who was born in Russia. At first he was quiet and listened carefully to everyone else talk. He was actually from St. Petersburg, Russia, and had emigrated to New York City at age 12. Obviously a bright kid, he quickly adapted languages and culture and found his way into a PhD program that specialized in planetary astronomy. In particular he studied meteor crater ejecta, which is the analysis of the matter blown out from meteor (and comet) encounters. On Mars there are many craters, understanding their ejecta can tell the story about the mass and velocity of the offending meteor or comet. From this knowledge, the story the creation of the planet and in fact the solar system as a whole can be un-raveled. He also possessed a good amount of knowledge in geology which would be useful during the rotation.

Leah was an import from Louisiana with a specialty in biology. She also was working on her PhD with a focus on exo-biology. She would spend her time in the books as well as working the Green Hab. This contraption was used to grow plants hydroponically from waste water as well as filter the water for later use. This proved no easy task but eventually there would be the solution (no pun intended) to creating oxygen and food on the Martian surface. Leah had the skills and professional approach to handle the job. Considering that none of the other crew mates had her level of experience in these matters, she became invaluable.

Ingmar was from Denmark, where he worked for an aerospace company on satellite sub assemblies. With a PhD in astronomy and a great attitude, he would be the morale leader in the weeks to come. His astronomical background and knowledge of spacecraft propulsion systems would ignite the crew's imagination. Stephen was impressed at Ingmar's excitement regarding the rotation. During the first evening they would talk about electronic cameras and digital measurement techniques, insofar as Stephen had several questions on these subjects. Ingmar was generous with his knowledge and when unsure would find answers from others in his field via e-mail.

So far the crew appeared to be unusually ego-less and Sally added to the chemistry with a keen mind focused on the orderly solution of problems. She obtained her PhD from Oxford in geo-physics at an early age and had continued a fine level of work as a scientific journal referee. As it would turn out, Sally would lead the geology experiments with the same high level of organization and scientific objectivity.

As for Stephen, he was best described as autodidact. Although having a significant amount of university experience, studying philosophy and later astro-physics, his life path found him working at several national laboratories including the National Bureau of Standards, National Center for Atmospheric Research and National Oceanographic and Atmospheric Administration. His duties typically were participating in small think tanks and tiger team groups designated to find unique and potentially patentable solutions to difficult technical problems. He had also taught radio astronomy at a local university. This subject had always been his favorite and led him to building several large telescopes and receiver systems. These systems included the use of two 18 meter diameter parabolic dishes and the building of several very large (300 meter +) phased arrays. Fundamentally, Stephen was an engineer and had a penchant for thinking up unique solutions to technical problems. On the side, he enjoyed flying airplanes and helicopters. At one point he had become a test pilot for a major airline, flying most of the large simulators to test and qualify the flight management computers.

The crew as a whole became a different organism when together however, and Stephen found himself in an intellectual vortex looking for an ignition source. Late night discussions would provide the ignition and their lives would be changed forever. For now however, Stephen would have to fix the plumbing, wiring and solar energy systems. Reality was starting to "bite".

Chapter 2: Ignition Source

"So far, so good"

The EVA team returned from a four hour trip to Goblin Canyon, hot, sweaty and tired.

"That was a long trip, but we got our prize," exclaimed Sally. As the spacesuits were being taken off, she showed the rest of the crew the spoils. Ten kilograms of emerald sandstone with several veins of gypsum embedded in it.

"These are the remnants of an ancient seabed that was

here 135 Million years ago. Check it out," said Sally. "This is the first piece of the puzzle that will let us know about the history of this area. We'll bring in the next piece tomorrow on your EVA," she announced. The EVAs were made up of three crew members going out per day. The others would help in preparation and tend to the hab during the day. The radios would also be monitored for any traffic. After suit extrication, the crew went upstairs for candy bars, coffee and a debriefing. This would be followed by dinner and report writing. All told, everyone was busy until at least 10:00 pm. The only break would come after dinner was finished when the crew could talk freely about anything. The typical conversation was about the voyage to Mars. This included the inevitable questions:

"Would you go if given the chance?"

"What science should be perform first?"

"What will it be like once it has permanent residents?"

Although philosophic in nature the questions would be answered in more scientific ways.

"Would you go if given a chance?"

"Of course, but we need to consider the human needs in terms of food and water."

"We also need to have a return voyage."

"Maybe initially, we should send robots to build structures and extricate oxygen from the atmosphere."

18

Mars Life

One evening, the conversation after dinner turned to the propulsion system required for a voyage to the Red Planet.

"How long will it take to get to Mars?"

"Six weeks to six months depending on the thrust of the rocket engines." Ingmar would explain that for a chemical rocket, like the Space Shuttle or Saturn Moon rocket, enormous amounts of energy is expended over several minutes to escape the earth's gravitational pull. In space there are a few more choices.

"You can still use chemical rockets, but you could also use nuclear, ion or solar. These devices must however be carried to or built in space. Some are much more efficient in terms of their output or specific impulse. You see, chemical engines can attain specific impulses of 500 seconds whereas ion engines for instance are capable of between 10,000 and 400,000 seconds. The only problem is that the thrust from a ion engine is small compared to the duration it can sustain power and quite the opposite in a chemical rocket. The ion engine is the winner in terms of speed, efficiency and economy (this is from Freeman Dyson).

"So why don't we use just the ion rockets?" asked Leah, "it seems to make perfect sense."

"Well, because the thrust is so small, we can't

escape gravity, so the only useful thing to do is use them in space," explained Vasili. "You see they are designed to accelerate small masses to a very high velocity using electromagnetic coils and other components found in vacuum tubes. In space you don't need the tube, just electricity and a supply of gas, typically Xenon."

Sally then asked, "But Xenon is not that heavy of an element on the periodic chart, wouldn't the engine be more efficient if the gas were much heavier? Actually, lets find a periodic chart and figure this out properly."

Vasili was the first to find one and report that Xenon had an atomic weight of 131.

"What is heavier?" asked Leah.

"Well there are many, but the one I would suggest is lead, which as an atomic weight of 207. The biggest advantage however is that it can be stored in a very compact way at room temperature. It will melt at 327 degrees C and boil at 1,740 C," observed Ingmar.

"Xenon on the other hand melts at -119 degree C and boils at -107 degrees C. It seems to me that we could store a significantly greater amount of lead than Xenon, and it would not require a pressure vessel."

"So," asked Stephen, "how do we make a gas out of lead, burn it?"

"Actually you could use a laser to boil off small

amounts of it and then accelerate the molecules out the rocket nozzle," interjected Sally. The atmosphere quieted as each crew member wondered why such a concept would not work. It was simpler and the amount of fuel that could be carried would be much higher.

Obviously, it was intriguing but the silence was soon shattered by Commander Benny.

"Reports, we are supposed to be doing reports. We can talk more after we finish our duties."

They all sat down at their respective lap tops and finished up the EVA, geology, engineering and command reports. Minds idled on the creative idea of a new rocket engine, however Stephen felt that something special was about to happen. This crew was the most intellectually capable he had ever worked with (and there had been some very good ones). As he typed out the voltages and water levels, graphed the usages and predicted fill up requirements, Stephen knew that upon rare times a group is capable of having a "logos" experience. This was a philosophic term used by the pre-Socratic Greeks to denote a flash of insight that "floats between the thinkers, as to be seen objectively by both."

"This was fun, how far could it go?" thought Stephen.

Every once in a while historically, there are these

21

groups of thinkers that create ideas and act on them to create something interesting. One of the more famous meetings was with Percy and Marie Shelly, Victor Hugo, and Bram Stocker. This happened in the late 1800's in Europe. They were all writers and poets and had an idea late one evening to create books about human aberrations that would terrorize the local population. The results were Frankenstein, The Hunchback of Notre Dame and Dracula. It was a creative revolution at the time and to this day is copied in literature and film. But, was this a similar occasion? Were these musing at all important? There were a lot of gaps and for the most part people get bored easily. Time would tell. As Stephen finished his reports, he wondered how important an invention like a lead ion rocket could be. If it worked it would revolutionize the rocket industry, but useful only to those scientists interested in interplanetary flight. This rocket would not be too useful on earth, you still need a lot more thrust to break the bonds of gravity. When in space however, this invention could propel a vessel far faster for far longer than anything else had. This plus simplicity and safety, what a combo!

One by one, the crew members finished their respective duties and sat back to relax. These were not easy days, although rejuvenating in a sense, work was done until late in the evening and little time was left to relax. But for these people, it seemed ok. It seemed that they, like water finding it's own level, lived in this way and as a result would become very accomplished. Being too tired to continue the logos, they one by one turned in and went to sleep. Stephen, somewhat energized by the experience started taking notes.

Chapter 3:   Combustion

"We now have locked onto the right stars and are on course"

Another day dawned, breakfast was served, minds cleared and the day's EVA was discussed. Stephen and his crew were off this day. During the crew meeting, he had several engineering details he needed to attend to. This would consist of evaluating the solar cell run green house and closely examining the plumbing.   Scotty from the

Mars Life

Enterprise never had to work on the plumbing, but this was real life.

As the lists were drawn and the plans laid out, the crew started the preparations. Initially, this would include the "off" crew assisting the EVA crew in donning their space suits and preparing their equipment. For the EVA crew this was enjoyable. The "off" crew would help them with the backpacks, water tubes, radios, GPS equipment, and PDAs. This all required taping and adjusting and testing and finally the attachment of a nail or other type of stylus to enable a suited crew member to push buttons and take notes. This was not a trivial task considering being inside a bulky spacesuit with thick gloves. During EVA, the suit and gloves stay on, unless of course there is an emergency. So the "astronauts" felt completely in "sim" and from this viewpoint could better understand the sensations astronauts and cosmonauts felt as they tried to perform tasks in space.

After suit-up the crew members gathered their geological gear consisting of hammers compasses and sample bags, then entered the airlock. A pressurization cycle of five minutes was imposed to make sure the outside and inside pressures were equal. This was really done with just a timer. Then upon the ding, the crew members exited and found their ways to the four wheel ATVs. These vehicles were used to drive to the site Sally or Vasili had chosen that would yield the most interesting geological specimens as well as for the next piece of the puzzle. An off duty crew member would perform a "pre-flight" to insure that the ATVs were in proper working order.

Actually, the work was harder than expected, the bulky suits inhibited movement and the temperature inside grew as the crew climbed up and down hills, ravines and valleys. A crew member learned to regulate his or her pace. This would allow the completion of the primary missions for that day. Many pounds of samples were returned. Later they were examined chemically and with a microscope. And of course photos were taken and reports written.

The discussions about the rocket engine continued, more on the level of understanding the details than on a theoretical level. The crew simply were doing the work to find out if the concept would actually work.

"How much electrical power is required to accelerate the lead molecules?" asked Leah.

"How is the lead to be vaporized?" asked Benny. These questions were worked out and soon Stephen found himself making drawings and having them reviewed by fellow crew members.

"The plumbing has to look like this to get the plasma ported properly out of the nozzle."

"Here is were the electrical coils need to be to

optimize output flow," Stephen remarked.

Late one evening, on about the fourth day of rotation Benny sat back from the discussions, reviewed the crew from a few meters away and remarked, "Everyone seems to be thinking this thing could work. We all have been sitting around doing calculations, drawings and planning for building a prototype. Are we really going to do this?" This caused the crew to stop and think for a moment. They had skipped a few steps along the way in terms of reality checking their actions. Instead they had taken on the task and using their intelligence and experience, starting solving problems like scientists and engineers characteristically do. No one asked about money for the parts or if it should be sold or patented. No one asked if it should be built in a certain country or how the management team should set up the proper sequence of meetings. All of the inefficiencies of modern aerospace engineering were absent. The true workers were just proceeding towards completion without any "overhead" or "support structure" or "burden". Although Stephen was the first to think philosophically about this, is seemed that with this group, the project was the purpose for living. It appeared to be a relief working without the encumbrances everyone was used to.

"Yeah, lets build this thing," Stephen said.

"If we can do our jobs here for the rotation, order parts and build a prototype it would be a great accomplishment. Think about it, even if we fail everyone would have learned a great deal about the fundamental problems of sending a ship to Mars. In fact, we are doing the quintessential work for a manned mission.   These questions have to be answered, and everyone of us will be better prepared to discuss the details. I think it is a great exercise, and oh by the way, what if it works, even partially? What if it is only 1% better than current engines? Listen, I tell you what, I will purchase the parts, UPS them into the closest gas station, on my non EVA days, I will retrieve the parts and we can just see how it goes. What to you think, fearless leader?"

"Well I don't know," thought Benny, "I have to justify the time spent on this as a worthy endeavor for us. It has to be directly related to our activities. I suppose that if we thought of ourselves on Mars and having to design a method to get home because something broke that would be reasonable. We have to accomplish all of our normal tasks as a first priority then work on this in the time left."

A moment later Benny added, "if we could do this in sim, meaning that we have to put on the suits, go somewhere for the outdoor testing that would be best. Let's do what we can in our time remaining." Fearless leader had spoken.

62.5 Milliseconds later, everyone spoke at once, bringing their respective chairs up toward the table. Activity was now at a serious pace. The crew felt released and responsible for completing the prototype in the remaining few weeks of the rotation. Quickly a list was written up for the first wave of parts. This consisted of aluminum tubing, spools of wire, ceramic parts, aluminum sheets, electrical connectors, a fish scale, insulators, capacitors, resistors, an oscilloscope and various small hardware pieces like screws and bolts. All told the list was for about 50 items. Stephen e-mailed his work mates back home and asked for expedited delivery to a gas station located several miles from the hab. A Visa card number was given and the e-mail sent.

It turns out that the design was relatively low risk. Internet downloads revealed the basic components of an ion engine. Several Nasa reports had detailed schematics the crew could examine and modifications were made from these designs. The main issue was how to release the lead ions and molecules, funnel them to the accelerations chamber and from there to the rocket chamber. In the case of ion engines, there really isn't a rocket nozzle per se, it is more like an area in space that contains the magnetic fields correctly positioned to accelerate the molecules and ions in a single direction. The general configuration has a propellant going through an ion source grid, the beam is then shaped by a circular electrode which is then followed by an accelerating electrode (again circular) and finally through a neutralizing electrode that adds the opposite polarity ions to the plasma flow. Another configuration is called a magnetron type bombardment ion source where an electron tube design (initially from radars in the second world war) is used to accelerate particles through a charged grid. These designs are relatively simple but all have the requirement of needing to operate in a vacuum. The first fundamental design was chosen, calculations were then made to accommodate the heavier ion and molecules. The most challenging part of the system was the electrical source. The greater the voltage and amperage the greater the flow rate and thus more acceleration. Stephen had built a propulsion system based on the Biefield-Brown effect whereby a large electric voltage was placed between two asymmetric capacitive plates. The system worked without a vacuum and calculations were made to indicate how to implement both ideas into one optimized system. As far as the electrical power source was concerned, solar cells could provide enough energy to propel a vehicle of this design. The output of the solar panels would be stepped up to millions of volts and then applied to the engine. The final design was an engine about one meter in length, 30 cm in width weighing 11 Kilograms. The output thrust in a vacuum was calculated to be 40 Kilograms. But more importantly, the output velocity was predicted to be 70% the speed of light. Einstein would have been impressed.

"The parts are ordered, the momentum is great and everyone is excited," Stephen reported to Benny.

"Let's see how it goes," Benny said before turning in for sleep.

Chapter 4: Balancing

"In two days we will have to start the de-acceleration procedures, we are going faster than predicted"

Two more days went by, the crew performed EVAs, wrote reports, and assembled the engine. More parts were ordered and preliminary tests of power supplies and sub components were made. During one of the EVAs, a sandstone cave was discovered in a remote area but still within reasonable distance to the hab. The walls of the cave were of a much denser material than the outside sandstone . Vasili suggested that some of the testing of the rocket could be performed inside the cave.   A partial vacuum could be obtained if the opening and floor could be sealed.   Ingmar concluded that aluminum plates and a welding machine should be used to seal the entrance, floor and any leaks in the walls. Stephen was somewhat familiar with welding aluminum and plans were made to purchase and send all of the necessary material. During the off days, Stephen worked on the cave, it had the advantage of being high enough in the hills to be both remote and having a good view of a valley to the east. This could come in handy if there had to be some secrecy exercised during the building of the prototype. The cave walls were indeed very dense, like granite or some other metamorphic type of rock. The inside dimensions were about 10 by 10 meters with a roof about as high. The floor was flat enough to bring in aluminum plates , weld them together and have them stay in place.   The walls also made it easy to place the plates around and seal. 32 plates the size of a common dining table were used. The welding went well and any suspicious joints were re-worked.   The vacuum needed to test the prototype did not need to be great, just enough to simulate a 20 Km altitude. This according to the calculations would be enough to create a stable, albeit low power rocket exhaust. Stephen worked on the room for about four "off" days and sealed it for another day before adding a sealed door made also of aluminum plate. To test the design, Stephen placed a barometric sensor inside and one outside for comparison. He had worked on meteorological sensors in a past occupation and had several extra sensors with the equipment he brought in from Colorado. A small hole was drilled into the side of the access door for the electrical leads and then sealed with epoxy. Stephen would watch the changes of the inside pressure versus the outside to determine how well the room would work. Meanwhile, he would order a vacuum pump from a catalog and have it delivered to the gas station. After connecting the barometric sensors to a PIC processor and recording the results for several days, it was determined that the room, although not perfect would suffice for the experiment.

"How is it going with the chamber," asked Benny.

"Well, so far so good, the pump should be here tomorrow and we will try to pump the room down to 10 e-8 Torr to see how well it works. I expect a little leakage but if we put the best vacuum on it, we should still have a few minutes to test the rocket before the pressure goes up. But I am surprised at how well it is now isolating the barometric pressure variations, I can't see any inside change," explained Stephen.

"I think Vasili, Ingmar and Sally are close to finishing the rocket, they have been working on 4 hours of sleep a night. Time is getting close for our departure so its going to be now or never," said Benny. "I feel comfortable enough to allow the final assembly of the rocket in the cave starting tomorrow if you want. I can still seal any minor leaks with epoxy as we move in," offered Stephen.

"Ok, lets do it," said Benny.

The next morning, the prototype engine was boxed and taken to the cave. Wires were attached through more holes drilled through the door. The fish scale was attached to a lever arm that would deflect if there was any thrust produced by the rocket. It was designed in such a way as to divide the real thrust by 10 then the indicator needle of the fish scale was attached to a potentiometer which in turn was attached to wires leading through the bulkhead. A simple ohm meter would register any deflection and one of the crew members would observe and record the results. After the_components were placed into the cave, the door was sealed and the newly arrived vacuum pump was attached to a fitting on the bulkhead. The pump was started and after a few hours, a vacuum was produced. Stephen turned off the pump and closed the vacuum valve to see how the system was working. He heard a hissing sound from a few places near the door attachment point and with some judicious placement of duct tape was able to quiet the chamber down. After a 15 minute test period, the vacuum gauges had barely moved. Although crude, Stephen was proud of the results and went back to the hab that evening feeling excited about the impending first rocket firing test.

"The chamber seems ok, it held 10 e -8 tonight for at least 15 minutes. If you guys are ready we can try to test fire the engine tomorrow?" said Stephen.

"We are running out of time," interjected Sally. "I tell you what, tomorrow I'll stay here and write reports for all of us so you can skip the EVA and work on the rocket."

"When you get back you can review the reports and make changes, I will base them on the work you have done so far," offered Leah.

"That would be greeeeat," said Vasili, mimicking a manager in the movie Office Space. Everyone laughed at this and decided to turn in early this evening.....it was only midnight.

The next morning, Ingmar woke up first, making coffee for everyone. Stephen was next up and opened up a package of instant breakfast to start the day. The others soon followed and plans were made for the test.

"We will need to finish the wiring and attach the high voltage power supplies first," said Ingmar. The power supplies were scavenged from several monitors that had been under the hab. These could provide up to 15,000 volts for the ion rocket. Other smaller supplies were also to be used for the filament and test probes to be used.

"I will place my camcorder in the chamber to record the exhaust and sounds," said Stephen. As far as the lead molecule source was concerned the crew had decided to heat a small lump of it on a hot plate and , with a CO_2 laser borrowed from one of Leah's laboratories, start burning bits off to be sent by pressurized gas to the rocket chamber. The apparatus was crude but in test runs the lead "gas" seemed to be constrained nicely inside the rocket nozzle. The final prototype weighed about 15 Kg, a bit off from prediction but still within reason. Vasili calculated that if the unit produced 50 Kg of thrust as measured by the fish scale, the unit would have proved the concept.

"So, here's the deal, Sally. I have rigged up the ohm meter to indicate one ohm for every 10 Kg of thrust produced by the rocket," instructed Stephen.

"Your job, should you choose to accept it, will be to record the ohm meter readings as well as anything said by the test operator which will be Ingmar. He will say things like 'High voltage on' or 'gas injector on', those kinds of things. It will be important to know how much thrust is being produced as Ingmar changes voltages or turns things on," said Stephen.

"Ok, Stephen , no problem," said Sally.

After breakfast, the crew quickly boxed the

equipment and drove the ATVs to the cave. Work proceeded rapidly and before lunchtime the placement of the engine and wiring was complete. The door was again shut and sealed. The bulkhead wiring was also sealed and the pump down was commenced.

"Considering all of the new wires in the bulkhead and the extra junk we put in the chamber, I think that we should let it pump down for three to four hours before the big test. We could go back to the hab for lunch and help Leah with the reports," said Stephen.

"Sounds reasonable," said Benny.

They returned to find Leah working on the reports and sending e-mails. They sat down to a meal of tuna fish with noodles and peas. A meal like that would be revolting for many people back home, but after working so hard and being out in the middle of nowhere, it was delicious.

"Bravo on the cooking," said Sally.

"Exemplary," added Vasili.

After lunch, work commenced on the reports. Leah had done a nice job in re-writing older reports to include new findings or amplify remarks already made. She tried to emulate the writing styles of the authors and did a reasonable job. After just another hour most reports were polished and sent to Mission Control back in Colorado. They seemed satisfied and probably thought 'this crew is maybe not the best ever but certainly competent'. The crew then gathered for one more meeting before the first test firing. As they were all scientists, they approached the test with the knowledge of many other tests done in each of their pasts. This meant that there had been successes and failures. They knew that if it did not work, the best thing to do was to understand why and try to improve the rocket to try again. Every once in a while things do go right, however they all knew that Murphy's law was all powerful. It was interesting to note that none of the crew members asked whether or not the thing would work. All were prepared for a possible failure and of course hoped for a success, of any sort.

"Ready?" asked Benny, "It has been more than three hours. How about we go out there and see how the pump down is going, set up our measurement gear and give it a try?"

"Absolutely," said Vasili. "Make is so," Star Trekked Benny.

The crew again gathered equipment and parts and drove out to the cave. The pump down had proceeded well and most of the vacuum seals had held. Wires were attached to ohmmeters, power supplies, and other recording gear. Places to sit were found, notebooks opened and written in. After another 45 minutes the time for the first test was upon them. As with other good scientific tests, procedures were followed that broke down the test into simple definitive movements. Ingmar was the official test conductor and as a result had the best place to sit. No one sat too close to the door or bulkhead, in case of trouble. Leah sat 10 meters to the left on the ground with the ohmmeter in front of her and a notepad on her lap. Vasili would monitor the power supplies and note any anomalies. Sally would observe the vacuum gauges and barometric sensors to watch for changes. Benny and Stephen would observe anything else including sounds and temperatures inside the chamber.

Ingmar in a professional voice said, "Ok, what I am going to do is take one step at a time. As I ask for a switch to be thrown, a measurement to be made or a power supply to be adjusted, I need you to repeat the instructions and confirm that you have done that action. Does everyone understand?"

The crew all acknowledged and braced for the test.

"Vacuum setting?"

"10 e - 9 and holding steady."

"Power supplies?"

"All off and standing by."

"Thrust reading?"

"Zero ohm, zero Kilograms."

"Temperatures?"

"All temperatures nominal."

"Camcorder?"

"Camcorder on and recording."

"Turn on the Beam Shaping Electrode power supply."

"Beam Shaping Electrode power supply on and steady."

"Accelerating Electrode power supply on."

"Accelerating Electrode power supply on and steady."

"Hot plate on."

"Hot plate on and voltage steady."

"Decelerating Electrode and neutralizer power supply on."

"Decelerating Electrode and neutralizer power supply on and steady."

"Temperature rising on the hot plate."

"Noted, tell me when it gets to 300 degrees."

"Roger."

"Biefield-Brown accelerator on."

"Biefield-Brown accelerator power on and steady."

"Stephen, note the time and remark that all power supplies are now on."

"Roger."

"Laser power supply on, beam off."

"Laser power supply on and steady, beam off."

"Chamber temperature has risen 3 degrees."

"Noted."

"In case of a problem I want the Biefield-Brown device turned off first followed by the accelerating electrode supply."

"Roger that."

"Hot plate temperature is now over 200 degrees."

"Thank you."

"Chamber temperature is up 10 degrees now."

"Roger, I am sure that is normal."

"How is the vacuum reading?"

"Steady so far."

"Temperature is over 250."

"Roger."

"Chamber temperature is 20 degrees above ambient."

"Roger."

"Hot plate temperature is now 300 and regulating."

"Roger, lets wait until the chamber temperature levels off before we proceed."

"Ok."

"Chamber temperature is now 40 degrees over ambient and stabilizing."

"Roger that, lets wait a few more moments."

"Chamber temperature is now steady."

"Roger that, Stephen note that all temperatures, pressures and voltages are stable, and include the time."

"Got it."

"Ok now lets open up the lead chamber valve and everyone watch their equipment very closely."

"Roger."

"I have a thrust reading of a few Kilograms a bit unsteady."

"Chamber temperature is up 20 more degrees."

"How are the voltages?"

"Steady, no problems."

"Ok lets turn on the laser and see what happens."

"Laser Beam High voltage switch coming on."

As the last procedure was enacted there was a high pitch whine heard from inside the chamber, in a few moments it was joined by a low rumbling sound. Every measurement device starting changing rapidly as did the reports.

"Chamber temperature rising very rapidly!"

"Thrust at 40 Kilograms and rising rapidly!"

"High voltage power supplies fluctuating!"

"There is smoke coming from the vacuum pump exhaust!"

"Ingmar! Thrust is over 180 Kilogram and climbing the meter can't keep up with the rate of change!"

"Chamber temperature up 200 degrees!"

Within a span of 12 seconds, the whine and rumble had increased by a factor of 10, with a slight hint of ground movement. All of the crew member changed their feeling from excitement to fear.

"Power supplies are really fluctuating badly!"

"Chamber temperature up 320 degrees!"

"We are loosing the power supplies!"

"Let's shut it down. Turn off the laser!"

"Biefield-Brown device off."

"It's off."

"Accelerating electrode power supply off."

"Roger that, electrode supply off."

"Laser off."

"Roger, laser is now off."

"Ingmar, there is a lot of smoke coming from the vacuum pump exhaust now."

"Roger, lets continue to shut it down and let it cool off; All power supplies off."

"Power supplies off."

"What is the thrust now?"

"Backing down to zero, there was a little bump on the way down."

"Roger, how about the temperature?"

"Temperature returning to normal, now 270 degrees and falling."

"Laser power supply off."

"Laser power is now off."

"Ok, lets just watch all of the instruments, let me know when the temperature is below 100 degrees. Also, everybody needs to start writing down what happened with a time line. We will let the vacuum pump expel the smoke and then we will turn it off for an inspection. Assuming the temperatures are down to normal."

"Ok."

"Ok."

The crew relaxed a bit and starting taking notes. Stephen and Vasili wandered around looking at the gauges, vacuum pump exhaust and felt the door for heat. It had been an exciting experience, no one knew if the thing was about to blow up, but they all were relieved when the order came to shut it down. It had started thrusting a lot sooner than expected and had gone way beyond the calculated levels. The temperatures rose initially as per calculation, but then there a run away condition initiated.

As the crew finished their notes, they rose and gathered around the door awaiting a look inside the chamber to see what had happened.

Mars Life

"That was not expected," understated Vasili.

"No kidding, this thing ramped up really quickly and produced a least a magnitude more thrust than expected," said Stephen.

"I think is was more than a magnitude," said Leah, "this thing was really cruising!"

After about 15 more minutes, Leah reported that the chamber temperature was descending below 100 degrees. The smoke was starting to clear from the vacuum pump exhaust. After a short conference, Stephen and Ingmar decided it would be safe to open the door and look at the engine. The vacuum pump was shut down and a relief valve opened. After several minutes had passed the hissing stopped and it seemed safe to open the door. Everyone crowded around the chamber as the door locks were loosened and the door handle pulled. The door opened a bit heavily as smoke poured out of the upper door frame. The inside light was illuminated and one by one the crew members entered. The first thing they noticed was that the engine was not in the same place they had left it but half a meter to the side. The steel and aluminum rocket stand had been deformed away from the exhaust port. Wires were frayed or charred, everything was black and sooty.

"Man, look at this place!" exclaimed Benny "It looks like a bomb went off in here."

"The camera looks ok but dirty," said Leah.   As Ingmar wandered over to the exhaust end of the rocket he turned 180 degrees and found in the dim light, a half meter hole where the exhaust plume would have been pointed.

"Hey everyone, come here," he said, "And bring a flashlight." Benny brought over a large flashlight, one that had a powerful beam.   "Look at this," said Benny, "What on earth happened here? And look, I can't see the end of the hole."

They crowded around the hole, used the flashlight to peer into it and found that it ran so deeply into the mountain that they could not see where it ended.

"This is unbelievable," said Ingmar, "And the walls are very smooth and parallel. This engine produced a beam that was at least as collimated as a laser beam. The energy that is required to make a hole this size in this rock can have only been produced by an apparatus working at near 100% efficiency; I can't believe that we could have done that with our crude setup. What did we do wrong, or right for that matter?"

The crew became quiet and all were wondering how this could have happened. The calculations were textbook, the design conservative and the support equipment crude. Some other un-explained physical phenomena had taken place. This would take a while to figure out. The decision was made to record everything with cameras, take more notes and seal the test cell up until the next day. It had grown late and the sun was going down. All they needed now was for some distant camper to see lights emanating from a distant hill side. A potential discovery of this magnitude would require secrecy. So they were careful to extinguish the lights, seal the door well, cover up tracks and go back to the hab using two different trails.

On the way back Stephen thought to himself, "Let's see now, we designed a rocket engine that maybe just maybe could produce twice the thrust of a normal proven design but ended up with a device that not only produced at least 10 times the amount, it also drilled a hole in a solid rock mountain side with the precision of a laser beam. Something doesn't make sense, especially with this highly competent group; these are all scientists that don't play games or take chances. Something very interesting has occurred today."

They met back at the hab and sat down for dinner and discussions about the day's event. All were completely surprised by the extra thrust the device put out. They were also surprised by the beam that drilled a hole in a mountain seemingly with ease.

"The calculations do not make sense," remarked Vasili, "the only way we could have produced a collimated plasma beam with that level of power would be if the ion engine worked at least 95% efficiency and the Biefield-Brown device collimated the beam as well as amplified the ion engine's output. Actually, we are probably incredibly lucky, this thing could have gone critical and blown us all up."

"I agree," stated Ingmar, "The numbers point to great efficiency and some how we stumbled on a plasma amplifier design that worked the first time. This is not normal in science. I think that we need to be very careful in how we record the results, it has to be done in such a way as to allow other scientists to replicate this engine in other labs. If it can be replicated, we will have produced a significant advancement in rocketry."

"Wait a minute," cautioned Benny, "We need to think about this. I agree that the increase in output thrust is a major achievement but I am greatly concerned about the other phenomena. What if this thing could be used to blow up buildings or hurt people. I mean think about it, we did this for a few thousand dollars, anybody could replicate it."

"I don't know," offered Leah, "I see your point but you might be a little too concerned about the harmful effects it might have."

"Actually, I kind of agree with Benny," countered Ingmar, "We need to be very careful about this thing, the only other device I know of that is capable a drilling a hole in a mountain side is a chemical laser and it typically is very large and definitely very expensive but remember our device required a vacuum to operate. We have something unique here and we have to be extremely careful in how we let our secret out."

"I agree," added Stephen, "But first let's do a very careful examination of the hole and rocket apparatus. We need to get a better handle on how much thrust it really did produce. We can do that by examining the rocket stand, which by the way I did briefly. It looks like we bent some metal and broke the fish scale. Let's be extra observant tomorrow and I think that after our examination we should dismantle it and clean the place up."

"Agreed," announced Benny, "But first we need to write reports about the EVA we didn't go on today. The crew smiled at this comment, cleaned up after dinner and began the process of writing fictitious reports. A few e-mails were sent to wives, husbands and kids. They were tired and emotionally spent. There was little time to think about the implications of this discovery. They retired to their staterooms at around midnight and slept soundly.

The next morning, the crew members arose to a beautiful day. Bright and clear with a slight chill as the sun rose. For the first time, they had actually slept in an extra 30 minutes.   Nonetheless they quickly ate breakfast and gathered their equipment and notebooks.

They made their way up to the cave and found it undisturbed. Opening up the door, they entered and retrieved the camera for later viewing, cleaned off the wires for examination and measured the deflection in the metal parts of the rocket stand. Vasili and Ingmar examined the hole and by placing a tape measure in the opening found that the hole was over 23 meters deep with a smooth bore right up to the end. They also found that the beam had no discernible divergence. Normally with a laser, there is a divergence angle of about .5 degrees, which although not a lot, will spread out the beam and as a result the energy will diminish as you get farther away from the exit aperture. This engine seemed to be confining the beam somehow to increase the efficiency of the output. The depth of the hole also indicated that great heat and energy was produced over a short period of time.

As the other crew members worked diligently, Stephen went outside for some fresh air and to think about the engine. As he looked out from the front of the cave towards the east, he thought he saw a glint of light from a hillside a few kilometers away. He froze in place, hoping to see it again or at least talk himself into a possible reflection of the sun off of some gypsum, which was plentiful around the hills near the cave. Then he saw it again, this time it flashed a few times as he realized that someone was out there looking at the cave with binoculars or worse a rifle scope.

Chapter 5: We have company

"We have the trajectory we need and will enter the atmosphere over the North pole to start re-entry"

Stephen ran back into the cave, "We have company, someone is out there."

"What are you talking about? We are in the middle of nowhere," queried Vasili.

"I just saw a glint from binoculars or a rifle scope, it was too bright to be gypsum or glass," answered Stephen.

Mars Life

"Great," said Benny, reacting with definite disappointment. "We should get our equipment out of here and clean up the cave," he added.

Ingmar, also disappointed said, "I was hoping to get another test run out of this, we could use as much data as possible to really understand what we have built." The crew, slightly shaken, started to clean up and finalize their note taking at a brisker pace. Sally remembered that Stephen had a pair of binoculars at the hab and offered to go and retrieve them for confirmation about the visitor. Benny, in favor of getting the binoculars insisted on someone going with Sally, for safety. Stephen offered to go along, and leave the other scientists to finish the measurements and cleaning. They descended from the cave entrance and using a pair of ATVs returned to the hab. The fear factor set in to make Sally and Stephen nervous upon entering the building. Although they had locked the hab up with chains and pad locks, they still were careful in examining the lock for any signs of tampering. There was none and they quickly entered, retrieved the binoculars, locked up the hab and returned to the safety of the others. Upon their return, Sally started to scan the area for the visitor and found none. This knowledge did not dissipate any of the worries that the other crew members shared. It was obvious that something important was within their hands, and surely needed to be protected.

"Lets, clean up this mess and get out of here," Benny insisted. "Ok, we are nearly done, what are we going to do about the hole in the wall," asked Ingmar.

"Fill it with dirt and cover the remaining hole with the aluminum wall plates, then we will pile up more dirt in the cave opening and hope no one discovers this place for a few years," instructed Benny.   The crew cleaned out the remaining equipment, filled the hole and redistributed the dirt to hide the metal plates to at least a cursory examination by future passing explorers. They piled the metal parts and test equipment on the ATVs (some precariously) and slowly descended the hillside and returned to the hab.   After bringing in the important pieces of the engine and engine stand into the lab in the first floor of the hab, they (in a somewhat paranoid fashion) closed and locked the doors to the airlocks.

Again, dinner was served and as it turned out that they had worked furiously enough to have totally forgotten lunch. After the meal, one whose contents they would never remember, it was time to talk seriously.

"Ok, has anyone e-mailed anyone else about our discovery?   It doesn't matter who, I am not angry, it's just important to find out what happened so we can handle the problem," asked Stephen. No one spoke for about a minute (a long time under these circumstances).

"Maybe it is just a coincidence," suggested Sally. "What is going on around here? Everyone is stressed about a possible spy watching us work with a possible invention of whose nature we don't yet clearly understand, let's get a grip on reality before we start posting guards and loosing sleep."

"Fair enough," answered Vasili, "but it is too curious that as soon as we get excited about something that is potentially important to inter-planetary travel, weird things start to happen."

The crew members regardless of what was happening on the outside had to make some important decisions. The rotation was winding down, they had missed a reporting day, re-wrote reports from a previous EVA and were tired enough to take another day off. Mission control was not made up of idiots and soon would detect a problem. Zubrin was monitoring the reports as well and could soon start asking questions. Stephen got along pretty well with Zubrin back home and would not feel comfortable stretching a truth or worse lying about their activities. This rotation (as well as all of the others) was about developing procedures for the real mission to Mars. It was incumbent upon the crew members to take the work seriously and contribute to the knowledge base that would be the foundation of the real mission. NASA and other prestigious institutions followed the work of the crew members and project in general. It was after all, doing research into crew psychology and task development for a real mission. The benefits were enormous really, as were the various similar experiments in the Mercury, Gemini and Apollo eras. All of the astronauts and cosmonauts of that time were tested for their responses in isolation, under stress, and in close working quarters with another crew member. The Mars Desert Research Station furthered the research by examining various crew combinations, with various problems to solve with finite resources. In the real flight to Mars, these people will be chosen very carefully. Experience in a rotation at the MDRS could be invaluable, teaching every member of the crew about their strengths and weaknesses. Which by the way include psychological, physical and philosophic. The first two of these parameters are easy to understand, with a great deal of work done in the past with crews going to the Antarctic (which by the way has been inhabited continuously for decades) as well as space. The interesting nuance comes in thinking about the philosophic implications of going to Mars. Unlike going to a space station or the Moon, going to Mars will actually be accomplished by scientists and pilots (no shock here) and pioneers. These pioneers, like those trekking across Oklahoma and Colorado westbound in the 1800s, will be staying in their new found land.   They will bring music, art, books, the sciences, religion to these environs.   There will be generations of these pioneers that stay on Mars, it will be quite a natural thing to do.

So the crew, knowledgeable about their potential important contribution to the Martian Mission, had to deal with the advancement in rocket technology but unfortunately with the fact that the invention could be used for harmful purposes.   And oh by the way, someone was possibly watching that could ruin the whole exercise.

"Ok, I have an idea," claimed Sally, "Lets get back to our normal procedures during the rest of our rotation and periodically go back to the cave to see if anyone is really interested in our activities."

After some thought, the crew members agreed. Stephen on the other hand agreed with the basic idea but was concerned enough about the potential spy to try to find out once and for all if it was a real problem. As Executive officer, he had a favorable position insofar as directing the crew during normal activities. He could use this leverage to find out if anyone had purposely or inadvertently let the outside world know about the invention. With discretion and a little creativity , he could discover if there was a real problem.   "Agreed," confirmed Benny with a nod from Stephen.

58

"Lets not shirk our real duties, we don't have a lot of time left here, let's make the best of it," Stephen added, "Ok, we are going back to our normal rotation of EVAs and I will assign an individual to make a quick check of the cave during that time."

The next morning, the EVA team consisting of Sally, Ingmar, and Benny suited up and chose an interesting geological site to explore. Stephen instructed Sally to spend a little extra time by taking the ATV up to the cave to check for intrusion and look around for glints or any other sign of observation. But just before Sally went to meet the EVA team to depart, he stopped her and told her to do the cave check first (unlike the previous plan to do it last). After the EVA the crew reported on their activities and Sally reported about her visit to the cave. Sally reported no glint or other sign of spy activity.

This went on for each EVA with Stephen assigning a different crew member the task of checking the cave. Stephen purposely would change the particular crew member's plans at the last minute regarding the examination of the cave. Unbeknownst to the crew member who where assigned the task of checking the cave, Stephen would use his binoculars to look over the cave area during the times he originally assigned to the crew member. In this way he could see if there were any messages going back and forth from a crew member that was informing their spouse et al about the activities regarding the cave. The logic was to imply to a potential spy that something important was going to happen at the cave and they should be watching it during that time. With Stephen changing the plans on each individual just before departure, this would allow him to observe a sign of someone monitoring their activities during the previously assigned cave examination time and deduce the reporting crew member. He assumed that a crew member was e-mailing someone about the activities and the e-mails were being transferred or intercepted. It would not take long to find out the truth.

After the third day of EVAs and mis-information, Stephen noticed dust from a vehicle around the original cave examination time. The dust was rising from the road that would come closest to the cave. The dust plume stopped at about the area where someone would have to stop and get out for a hike to finish the journey. It was Leah's day to examine the cave, which as it turned out she had done hours earlier when Stephen intercepted her to change the plan. So now Stephen was watching a potential spy following the script of mis-information. On a roll, Stephen decided to pre-position himself at the place of the glint sighting before this person arrived there to observe the crew. Stephen grabbed a radio, spare EVA suit and a notepad before leaving the hab to cut directly over to the spot. He reached the top of the hill, guessed at where the other person would set and maneuvered down to place himself in such a way as to be hidden until the other person chose his final viewing spot.

In about 10 minutes, Stephen heard the noise of someone lugging up camera equipment and other parcels. The person was breathing heavily from his efforts and soon stopped to catch his breath. After another minute of puffing the person picked up his load to make the final push to the observation spot. Stephen had chosen the position well and soon the person rounded a large boulder and froze as he saw one of his subjects, not a kilometer away but five meters. He starred at this person with the EVA suit on and was not in any place to make an excuse about his activities.

Stephen spoke first, "How ya doin?" No answer.

"Well, we been watching you for several days and just could not figure out what you were doing here; I mean there really isn't any wildlife to speak of and you seem to like this spot, kind of devoid of any geological interest. My name Stephen and if you want, I can call Mission Support to help you get some directions, would you like me to do that?"

The frozen, silent person finally spoke. "No, thanks ok I can figure out where I am now, thanks anyway."

Stephen continued, "Well judging from your

cameras and telephoto lenses, it looks like you are taking some pictures from a reasonable distance, say about a kilometer. It is kind of odd, there isn't much to look at around here. What are you up do?"

The person spoke quickly as he had already made a decision. "What am I up to? That's kind of sensitive. (he took a breath) In fact I am a prospector looking for new sources of fossils to sell. So I came to this, uh, Devonian formation to look around." A bad chess move on the part of the stranger.

"Well, sorry pal but this is Morrison formation all around here, and as far as finding fossils is concerned they are everywhere including that pile of fossilized bi-valves or bracia." Stephen pointed to the pile 10 meters away as he spoke.

"In fact If you want the Devonian period it's the next state over. There is a fossil outlet in town, I will call them so you can get better directions."

Caught in a lie, the person rose to gather his equipment and said, "No, again no thanks, I will just leave and explore somewhere else."

With that, he started down the hill and back toward the vehicle, probably to call his boss and tell him of his success. Stephen smiled with a smirk, and started back to the hab to tell the others and have a little conversation with

Leah.

"So Leah," started Stephen in front of the now assembled crew, "Who have you been talking to about our special work in the cave." Leah was embarrassed but said, "No one, just my husband and he would never tell anyone else, I was very specific in my e-mails."

"Leah, your e-mails went through an un-encrypted satellite link and over the Internet that is monitored 24 hours a day for key words and phrases," admonished Benny.

"Someone in Washington has a file on us now and is watching every move, they probably are doing background checks on everyone as well."

Leah, still embarrassed said, "Sorry I didn't realize how anyone could see what I was typing, sorry."

The crew quieted for a few moments. I became obvious to Benny that the only way out of this un-wanted scrutiny was to e-mail some mis-information and lead the onlookers to the path of boredom. "Leah," started Benny, "we are going to have to write some e-mails for you over the next few day, ones that will lead whoever is watching us astray. What time to you usually e-mail your husband?"

"Around 8 o'clock," reported Leah.

"My husband will know that I am not writing the e-mail if it comes from you guys."

"Well it won't," countered Stephen, "We are going to

give you some phrases and ideas to put into the e-mail that *you* will write. You have got to sell your husband on the idea that we failed, we in fact found out that our recording apparatus was completely bogus and the hole in the wall was already there, we just loosened some dirt. Tell him that we think that it was really a mine opening with an air shaft drilled into the side. And oh by the way, we need to review the e-mail before you send it."

"Ok," said Leah sheepishly.

She got to work and with a crew review and minor changes, sent her husband the e-mail. The crew would wait for a reply, then based on whatever her husband said, would lead him (and the others) away from the idea that anything worthwhile had happened. The e-mails, one or two per day went back and forth and the husband was certainly convinced that the test had been a failure. He showed definite disappointment but understood the story. After several days, it looked like they could back off, and with the little meeting with Leah felt that she could be trusted enough to not spill the beans. After all, the apparatus was torn down, and she was a medical person, not really understanding the physics of rockets and particle beams.

In the end the spy never came back and because it was time to get ready for the next crew, attentions was diverted from the experiment. On the final day of the crew's rotation, Stephen proposed a deal.

"I would like to continue the work we started here at my laboratory back home. I know that most of you are busy and can't put in the time necessary to finish the work. I have a pretty sophisticated laboratory and would be willing to share any of the work with you as it gets developed. If it turns into a product, I would propose sharing the profits from it's sale. What does everyone think?"

Sally spoke first, "I have no facilities to do anything more but I would like to see if it really is anything of worth."

Vasili added, "I agree with Sally, let's let Stephen continue and see what happens."

The rest of the crew nodded in agreement as they all felt the same way.

"What is a fair percentage?" asked Stephen.

"How about 10% for each of us and you get the remainder for spending your own money to complete it?" proposed Benny.

"Sounds good to me," said Ingmar.

All the others agreed and went back to packing and writing the final reports.

Chapter Six: Real work begins

"We are in the groove, everyone cinch up"

After the great experience working with great people and as a bonus creating something new, Stephen went back to Colorado to continue the work of building a second prototype. He had been successful in the design of special radar systems, and during the boom of the 1990s had sold his business and ended up with a lot of money and stock.

Mars Life

His family had been taken care of and their families to come. With the remaining cash and stock, Stephen wanted to do something significant. He and his wife created a foundation to help improve education for pre-school kids and Stephen started a project that was the culmination of 30 years of dreaming. As a young boy, Stephen had often wondered about how to make a vehicle that could fly and possibly break the earth's gravitational bonds and go into space. As he grew older, he discovered that it was not a trivial dream to satisfy. The brightest minds in the world dedicated their lives to this pursuit and it was very expensive. Currently, the Space Shuttle used a combination of solid and liquid fuels to take up to 100,000 pounds to orbit. Although an amazing engineering feat, it was not capable of going to the moon and beyond. During the 1960s and 1970s the Saturn rocket had taken a handful of astronauts to the moon. But after the Apollo 17 mission, the public was not so interested in continuing the effort and further moon exploration missions were canceled. Attention went to sending up communication satellites and sending robotic spacecraft to the planets. The mission to Mars grew more complicated after the Apollo mission was cut short. Robert Zubrin had correctly theorized that the technology was now present to pursue a mission to the Red Planet but the political climate had to evolve to allow this to happen.

Mars Life

The pioneer spirit was in most people and it was the next logical step for mankind. The space program had become very expensive, and a few accidents had diminished the willingness to take chances with human beings in space. A space station was being built that although a pared down version of the original design, was making progress in establishing an orbiting permanent presence in space. It too was very expensive. The will and desire were there for the forward thinking scientists of the time, but the constraints were daunting.

Stephen on the other hand, had correctly or incorrectly thought about the details of a mission to Mars and was willing to spend his money on an attempt. He spent time with Zubrin's engineers at his astronautics company. They educated Stephen about the requirements of rocket power and discussed terms like delta v and isp numbers. The laws of the universe were pretty stable regarding the necessary power and speed to take a vehicle from Earth to Mars. There were many options in terms of time of transit and how long you could stay on the planet. Zubrin's engineers, Mark and Gary by name were familiar with the atmospheric chemistry and what one could expect upon landing. Stephen had discussions with Zubrin and the engineers about as many details regarding the trip as possible. It all got down to one thing. What kind of propulsion would you use? If it was chemical, it would require a significant amount to take there and return. If it was solid, the same rules would apply, with the exception that it would not be throttle-able like the chemical types. As far as nuclear or ion propulsion was concerned, they made the most sense but would require assembly in space before the real trip could start. This sounded expensive. Zubrin had calculated that a refurbished Saturn rocket could leave the earth and go to Mars with an empty crew return vehicle, then using a robotic fuel generator, take the indigenous CO_2 atmosphere and produce enough rocket fuel to enable a crew, traveling in a second Saturn rocket crew capsule, to return safely to earth. The round trip would be on the order of two years. Although sounding like a long time, constant communications would be available through an e-mail link (of all things, just like and simulated by the hab in Utah) and this would allow the crew members to build greenhouses and other buildings to be ready for more explorers to come from earth. In this way and over a multi-decade period, Mars would be populated and become a home for many. The Zubrin plan had much merit and produced a great amount of interest, but with the exception of those who owned the Saturn rockets. It would be too risky to try they thought. New rockets needed to be designed and built, and this would take time; first of course the budget would have to be available to start this venture. This was a problem currently and would not go away easily.

Stephen thought differently about the whole concept. Zubrin's plan made the most sense with regards to the proclamation that the technology existed presently to allow such a mission to transpire. Stephen had another idea however regarding the vehicle of choice. In his business experience, Stephen had observed successful companies making great products based on assembling existing parts into something new. This was known in government circles as COTS or Commercial Off The Shelf equipment. In the commercial world, this was known as integrating. This reduced the engineering risks by having them create new products from proven sub assemblies. Stephen was in agreement with the philosophy and wanted to design an interplanetary vehicle from existing technologies. His idea was to buy an existing commercial aircraft and modify it to escape the earth's gravitational field and then propel itself to Mars. This craft would have to be big enough to house a crew of four, keeping them alive by providing water and food for a long period of time. It would also have to be pressurized to traverse the vacuum of space. It would have to be strong enough to land on Mars and then return to a landing on earth. After many conversations with Gary and Mark, Stephen had a vision of using a large commercial aircraft, fitted with auxiliary propulsion to be used in getting beyond the atmosphere and then a third kind of propulsion to enable it to go fast enough to make it to Mars in a timely fashion. As far as size was concerned, the largest aircraft available to adequately house the crew for such a long journey was a Boeing 747. There were quite a few sitting in "bone yards" that could be purchased and retrofitted. These were pressurized and had the ability to climb to 50,000 feet where the atmosphere was very thin and as a consequence would minimize the fuel required to enter orbit. They also could carry enormous loads and had gross take off weights over 800,000 pounds. Stephen thought about using the multitude of fuel tanks on board a 747 to house a minimum of jet fuel, water, liquid oxygen and other tank-able fluids for the journey. After more discussions with the engineers, he decided to use a chemical rocket engine to add additional thrust to the 747 at 50,000 feet to allow it to go into low earth orbit. A reasonable mixture of rocket fuel was kerosene and liquid oxygen. Jet fuel was essentially kerosene and could be used for the second stage of the flight. In addition, a series of smaller rockets placed around the airframe, called reaction control jets could use the same fuel. The combination of the main engine with the RCS (or Reaction Control System, which included the jets) the 747 would be transformed from an aircraft into a spacecraft. The problem would be in selecting the right engine. One capable of using the kerosene/oxygen fuel mixture, throttle-able and could easily be attached to the 747 airframe. Stephen again sought the advice of the rocket engineers, Gary and Mark.

Stephen asked, "Why don't we use a X-15 engine, it seemed to have the right features?"

Mark answered, "True, but it is too small for your application, that engine produces about 50,000 pounds of thrust where you will need much more to get your airframe into space. I would suggest the RS-23 engine from the first stage of a Delta II rocket. That should do the trick. It puts out over 200,000 pounds of thrust and can be vectored."

As usual, the advice was invaluable and with Gary concurring, Stephen started to study the use of such an engine a little further. First of all the Delta II rocket might weigh 100,000 pounds upon takeoff. This included fuel, airframe and payload. This was a bit lower than the proposed 800,000 pounds plus when the 747 achieved 50,000 feet. The engine would not be able to propel the aircraft at the same acceleration as the Delta II. The burn time would have to be longer, which would require more fuel, which would require more weight and complexity. Stephen studied the problem by drawing curves and using programs like Mathcad to calculate the point where the combination of rocket power and diminishing jet thrust would still combine to allow the aircraft to enter orbit. As it turned out the 747 ran out of "wing" before it ran out of "engine". In other words the wing came close to stall speed at these altitudes and the control surfaces could not handle the required aerodynamic forces necessary to keep the aircraft flying properly. The engines however were still producing thrust and would continue up to beyond 70,000 feet. Stephen reasoned that if the RS-23 was ignited and the RCS enabled at 50,000 feet, the aircraft would start accelerating, increasing the airflow into the engines; the RCS system would take over the attitude control and in this way the regular jets would produce thrust well above 80,000 feet. Beyond that point the jets would spool down due to lack of oxygen and eventually cease producing power altogether. The RS-23 engine however would be still producing 200,000+ pounds of thrust and would run at this level until the fuel ran out. Stephen calculated that the time required to go from 80,000 feet to 200,000 feet solely on rocket power was on the order of eight minutes. Stephen calculated the amount of propellants needed to finish the orbital insertion and found that it would be about 100,000 pounds of fuel. The 747s tanks held 347,000 pounds of fuel which would be more than enough for the kerosene part of the rocket propellant. The liquid oxygen on the other hand would probably have to be contained in the fuselage of the aircraft.

This would allow better insulation to be used and the proper components to be employed considering how cold liquid oxygen is. The empty tanks would be used for other things once the aircraft was in orbit. Stephen calculated that if the RS-23 did it's job to complete fuel exhaustion, the orbit that could be achieved would be around 100 nautical miles up. This was about the same height as the space shuttle could achieve.

The next step of course would be getting from earth orbit to Mars. To do this would have to include the new ion engine. Stephen knew that there were a few simple prerequisites, namely a lot of electrical power and an reasonable amount of basic fuel; this would be lead instead of Xenon. And he knew that extra equipment would be required beyond that of an standard ion engine. This would include several high power lasers and a lot of wiring. But first things first, the new ion engine needed to be finished and thoroughly tested. But even before that, Stephen needed a secure place to work, one where a Boeing 747 would not look out of place. This place would also need a multitude of airframe and power plant technicians who would not have any problem working on a classified mission (or so they would think). In addition, spare parts would have to be readily available, and it would be better to barter on the individual parts instead of filling out a ton of paperwork.

The best place then would be the aircraft "bone yards" near Davis-Monthan Air Force Base near Tucson, Arizona. This area preserves aircraft extremely well, has millions of parts, a good climate for continuing work in the winter time, and a plethora of aviation mechanics. Many a strange project has been built there and the technicians are used to having a "need to know" before asking too many questions. Stephen decided to break the entire project up into smaller separate projects separated by enough distance to keep technicians or engineers from talking to one another. As Stephen was a pilot he could fly between cities around the area to keep up with the progress of the individual tasks. Under the pretense of seeing his dad, Stephen would fly to Phoenix and back to Falcon Field and thence to Marana and finally to Davis-Monthan. These airfields were far enough apart to keep the "cross talk" down.

Stephen's first task was to procure a decent 747. One that was not beat up by freight operations or aged by thousands of Atlantic crossings. Also, the right version (called dash number by those in the business) that would have the best altitude performance. This would require an optimum combination of wing design and engine selection.

Mars Life

The Boeing 747 series is long and varied. General Electric, Pratt & Wittney, as well as Rolls-Royce had produced engines for the aircraft. There were 747-100s, -200s, -400s, Sps, and many special editions to choose from. Prices for the aircraft varied quite a bit, like a run out -100 freighter for about 10 Million dollars to a new -400 passenger airliner for 75 Million dollars. In terms of altitude characteristics the best combination seemed to be used passenger -400 with Rolls-Royce engines and an updated wing planform. Winglets had been added as well as subtle re-curvings of the wing surface to increase the fuel efficiency at high altitudes for these upgraded birds. The efficiency increase meant that the reserve thrust would be greater at high altitudes and could be used to get the ship as high as possible before the RS-23 would need to take over. With a little detective work, a used airliner was found that fit the bill, it was being fire saled by a major airline operation because of falling profit margins and competition from the newer Boeing 777. Stephen went to the company responsible for moving the aircraft and found (to his dismay) that the operations closely resembled a used car sales outlet.

"When in Rome.....," he thought. Negotiations began with the head salesman, who luckily did not care what the end use was; there were periods where Stephen threatened to get up and leave, followed by the lowering of price.   Back and forth they went for several hours after which the salesman had to see the color of the money before proceeding.   Stephen obliged with a conference call with his banker.   Satisfied, the salesman continued the negotiations until Stephen insisted on a stripped aircraft devoid of avionics and interior. This brought the price down further and in the end 22 Million dollars changed hands and the aircraft would be delivered to Davis-Monthan as agreed. The pretense was that Stephen's company was in need of a long range large transport for unusual freight operations. The salesman really did not care as he needed to make a sale badly. They shook hands and parted ways.

Stephen thought as he left, "I wonder what this character is going to think when he finds out we are going to Mars with this thing?" Smiling, Stephen waited for his prize to be delivered.

The next large task was to procure the rocket engine, also from Boeing.   This would be an entirely different type of negotiations. The Boeing sales team would be significantly more sophisticated than the used aircraft salesman he just left. They would be sincerely interested in the engine's final use. As it was used for low earth orbit insertion; the rocket it was attached to could also be used for military purposes. Buying this engine was not an "off the shelf" deal. But there was an advantage, Boeing made the

77

aircraft Stephen now owned as well. The strategy would be to tell Boeing about attaching the rocket engine in an attempt to enter low earth orbit. The numbers were there, and hopefully Boeing would be interested in seeing one their progeny achieve fame. Also , there would not be any question about the monetary capabilities of the company as well (Stephen ran all of his dealings out of a private company, named Hipparchos (after the first Greek astronomer)). Of course, there would be a sea of lawyers who would protect Boeing from any exposure due to mis-calculation or ineptitude on the part of Stephen's company. In fact, the smart thing to do would probably assure Boeing that 1) they could inspect the engine installation at any time and 2) the test flights would not be public knowledge, unless Boeing agreed that they were successful. Obviously, Stephen would not have a problem with that kind of proposal and hopefully, neither would Boeing.

Before the meeting in Seattle was to take place a few details needed to be ironed out. First the motor mount and thrust vector controls needed to be designed and operations simulated. Then all of the necessary support hardware needed to be identified and designed into the aircraft. This would include all of the plumbing, tankage, control systems, and any other mechanical hardware. Drawings needed to be made and calculations run, so

Stephen enlisted the help of a competent mechanical engineer with aerospace expertise, who lived in Phoenix. After five weeks the preliminary design was done. The engine would be attached below the horizontal stabilizer of the 747. It would have hydraulic actuators that would trim out the angle of exhaust exit to best propel the aircraft.

Aerodynamically, the drag was minimal and the engine was positioned along the centerline of the 747. Shrouding was added to further minimize this drag, including a tail cone apparatus that would be ejected right before the engine lit. It would float down to earth on a parachute and sink into the sea (as this is where the planned tests would take place). Fuel lines were run from the center tank of the 747 through high speed pumps to the engine and a liquid oxygen tank was added near the tail of the aircraft to provide the oxidizer. Weight and balance calculations were made and found to be acceptable if balanced with weight in the front of the aircraft. This would not be any problem considering the packing of the 747 with food, water and equipment for 1.5 years worth of living.

After the five weeks of design effort, Stephen was about ready to travel to Boeing. The aircraft also arrived in Tucson ready for outfitting. It was placed inside a large hanger and would remain there until finished and ready for a test flight. For now it was just another retrofit job as far as the locals were concerned. He contacted the appropriate sales person at Boeing, who of course was highly skeptical, but agreed to a face to face meeting. This took place a week after the phone conversation in Everett, Washington, inside the giant Boeing complex. The meeting consisted of Stephen on the one side of a large conference table and six Boeing personnel on the other. This was not going to be a cake walk, and the deal could fall through in moments if they thought that their time was being wasted.

"Good to meet you Stephen, thank you for coming up to see us," started the head salesperson.

"Thank you nice to be here," replied Stephen.

"As you know, this is a rather strange request you have of us regarding the RS-23 engine, there are of course several concerns we have. One of which was your financial ability to purchase such an engine but we received assurances from your banker that indeed that would not be a problem. That aside we can get down to the basics of responding to you request. You indicated over the phone that you were intending to attach this engine to a 747-400 airframe. You also indicated that you have a preliminary design for an engine mount and the required plumbing. We will have to review those plans of course."

"Understood, I have with me the drawings and calculations to enable your engineers to review our design."

"Good, now for the hard part, obviously we are in the business of selling rocket engines in this division of Boeing but we need to know exactly how they are used so if there is any chance that the engine could fall in the wrong hands there could be serious governmental consequences. Also, any un-authorized personnel handling this engine could present a threat as well. The State Department will have to be notified of your activities, do you have any problem with this?"

"None whatsoever, I fully understand your concerns," said Stephen.

"Maybe you do, and maybe you don't Mr. Daedalus," said the second salesperson.

"We could have serious legal exposure if anything goes wrong, especially over populated areas."

Stephen countered, "We are intending to conduct our tests in secrecy, with the exception of notifying Boeing, your personnel are welcome to observe the flight, and any other details regarding the testing. Also, our flights will be conducted solely over the ocean, near the equator to minimize the energy necessary to enter orbit."

"You will need to sign a waiver of all rights regarding the operation of this motor."

"I understand, no problem."

"Mr. Daedalus," said the third salesperson, probably

the manager of the department, "We will need to monitor all of your progress and will have our personnel present at all times during this project. But most importantly, if it works we will want to protect the design and use it for some other Boeing business that I am not at liberty to go into. Is this acceptable?"

Stephen did not expect to see the light at the end of the tunnel so soon, but understanding that obtaining the engine could only be accomplished by accepting the constraints of the Boeing company, he was obliged to accept.

"I can live with your rules and would be happy to work with your people," he said.

"One last rule," the manager added. "The work must be done here at the Everett facility."

We will use the same facility that is used to retrofit Air Force One and all personnel have secret or higher clearances.

Stephen was not prepared for this but after a moment of consideration again agreed to the terms.

"That will be fine."

"Good, my people will attend to the financial and scheduling details. We need the work to start soon as we have some time constraints regarding that other business I spoke of. Any of your people will need to be cleared with us and the FBI before they enter the facilities. You of course have already been checked out and insofar as you have had a secret clearance already, we will get that re-enabled. You know the drill, report to us next week for a security briefing and after that you can get to work. For simplicity sake we are going to hire you as a manager in our R6 department, everyone will leave you alone considering that. You will receive a badge and a paycheck starting next week. I have to go to another meeting now. Good doing business with you."

With that the manager rose, shook hands with Stephen and departed.

"You didn't have a chance unless you got by that guy," reported the first salesman. I understand that you will report directly to him and the section chief of the R6 department. Even the people in this room do not know what goes on in that department, only not to ask any questions or we will end up on someone's carpet. So I suggest you do the same starting the moment you leave this room. You will be contacted in the next day or two and it looks like you have an engine. Thank you for your business."

Everyone in the room rose to see Stephen out. During the meeting, several people there took notes and asked no questions, which was curious. It was interesting to wonder why all of the secrecy and apparent ease of getting such a prized piece of equipment, but he had work to do and wondering would just be a waste of time. Although it seemed the rules were about to change regarding daily operation, Stephen was more consumed with thinking about the details of moving the aircraft back to Seattle and finding new engineers to do the other details of the mission.

"Wait a minute," thought Stephen, "They didn't even tell me the price!" There would be many more surprises.

Chapter 7 : A new paradigm

"Airframe is heating up, 30 minutes"

Phone calls, meetings, visits, more phone calls, plane trips, and decisions were now the descriptive words of Stephen's life. On the fast track, sipping through a fire hose, all of the fast lane colloquialisms applied. Work was now at Everett with a crew of 30. All were disciplined and pre-screened or pre-chosen by the Boeing managers. With Stephen's management status and more importantly the color of his badge, all other personnel at the hanger would completely leave him alone, even to point of avoiding eye contact. Straight ahead walking, do your job, don't ask questions, everyone is listening. It took some getting used to, however the big decisions were being made regarding avionics, living quarters, fuel details, orbital dynamics, length of flight. As far as the flight was concerned, a significant amount of energy was put into the flight plan preparations. There were many meetings regarding contingency planning and how the risks were minimized by such things as thinking about when certain events had to happen.

At first glance, the flight plan looked like a jumble of commands regarding switch placement, flight control tests, flight system measurements. But upon further examination, the flight plan would dispense with the most dangerous tests while on the ground, moving into the least risky operations upon take off and finally into a flow of procedures that all had multiple safety backups.

The decision tree or matrix was understood after 1000s of man hours. The roots of the tree was made up of thousands of tasks, all extremely important, the tree diminished in size until the top of the branches, where there were but few operations, the final one being - open the door and step out. The Boeing crew was made up of very serious engineers and technicians all focused on one task.

This was in contrast to the MDRS crew in the sense that there was a lot of creativity shown by the MDRS people, their ideas were bold but risky. The crew at Boeing on the other hand, minimized risk at all costs and as a consequence scripted almost all activities during the flight. It was rather interesting to think that is would take both of these impressive yet antipodal groups to achieve such an ambitious goal.

They (the flight crew) would take the following equipment with them for the exploration of the planet Mars:

1. Greenhouse equipment for oxygen generation and eventually food.
2. CO_2 gas reactors to create oxygen and rocket fuel for the return trip.
3. ATVs capable of roving the Martian landscape for exploration.
4. Communications equipment to be left on Mars to relay weather information and habitat status. The habitat would be left to accommodate the next crew.
5. Balloons for the autonomous exploration of the surface over great distances.
6. Ground Penetrating radar equipment for the search for water.

7. Robots to do the tedious tasks of searching for water, construction of living habitats and maintenance of the habitat while awaiting a future crew.

8. Solar power panels to provide electrical power for all activities.

9. A fully autonomous visual and infrared observatory.

10. Wide band phased array radio astronomy observatory that would in addition transmit, for use in wideband communications and radar functions.

11. Astronomical sensor suite including x-ray, gamma ray, cosmic ray and ultraviolet detectors.

12. Surface sensor suite including seismic, magnetic, field mill, and gas chromatograph.

As far as the aircraft was concerned it was outfitted with closed cycle oxygen systems, water systems, solar cells along most of the fuselage, solar panel wings to be deployed once in space, multiple redundant navigation systems, redundant communication systems including laser modulators, comfortable living quarters including safe areas for the eventual high energy particle storms. Fuel cells for the production of water and electricity. Enough food rations for 2 years (now the rational for a craft the size of a 747 should now be more clear). Each crew member would be allowed 100 pounds of personal equipment. The outfit list was extensive and when added to the necessary fuel load, heavy.

The aircraft would be at full gross weight upon takeoff, after reaching altitude and navigating to the orbital insertion position it near the equator and would take on liquid oxygen from a airborne tanker, this would minimize the insulation requirement for the LOX tank and allow for the maximum payload weight upon the climb to orbit. After the jet fuel was partially used, the remaining tanks would be filled temporarily with LOX, the biggest being a fuselage tank in the rear of the aircraft. After the airborne fill up, preparations would be made for orbital insertion, again at full gross weight.

The crew was selected based on a multitude of factors, and each crew member would be evaluated from a physical and psychological standpoint. Stephen was allowed to go (seems funny considering he financed most of the project) because of his aviation experience. He would go as commander, a well respected test pilot, Benjamin Alas would go as pilot. The remaining two crew members would be scientists, made up of two women with significant NASA experience. The first, Judy Maimonides was a geologist cross trained in astronomy, the second Nanci Vico was a biologist cross trained in medicine. The two flying crew members, Stephen and Benjamin were both cross trained in engineering. This seemed like an optimal mixture of talents however in reality all crew members would participate in any task needed to complete a successful voyage.

After a year of preparation, for both the aircraft and the crew, a date was set for launch. The launch would be proceeded by several test flights initially with just the pilots; the last test flights would include all crew members and would focus mainly on safely procedures.

A week before the first test flight, Stephen was called into the office of the manager that had attended the first meeting regarding the Delta engine.

"Have a seat, Stephen," said the manager, "We have to talk." Stephen did as he as told, knowing finally who was really steering the ship.

"I have kept a careful eye on this project, and it is nearing the first test flight. I need to tell you about your additional duties upon orbital insertion. We have placed our best engineers on this project and the chances of you achieving your goal are quite good. But it will come at a price, Mr. Daedalus. As you know, we did not discuss the cost of the engine we bolted onto the airframe. Obviously it is worth many millions of dollars, but it turns out that it became a business decision to try your method of orbital flight as opposed to ours. We have spent several years exploring the requirements of sending large low earth orbiting satellites into orbit. As I mentioned the design of these satellites is none of your concern but you need to know that they will be carrying some potentially dangerous chemicals in the form of hypergolic solutions. Benjamin your pilot is fully familiar with the additional payload you will be taking up with you and will handle the deployment of these satellites. You will allow him to complete his mission. You will also not allow anyone including the other crew members to know about his activities. This will be especially true of mission control who by the way due to a suddenly sincere interest in your project, will be handled by NASA. The installation of the satellite deployment equipment is proceeding as we speak. As it turns out you will be saving us many hundreds of millions of dollars and if it works, will put 1200 engineers out of work. It's all about the bottom line you see. And as we have discussed in the past, if it does not work no one will know. We have only a few informed parties outside of R6 observing our activities, mostly in Washington, D.C. This is why you were not ejected from

91

our first meeting; someone thinks that you and your band of pin heads playing Martians in Utah were on to something. Maybe it has to do with some of Tesla's un-public work, who knows. But I do know this: you will follow the flight plan exactly as written. Because if you don't your mission will be terminated."

With that sobering news, Stephen arose and after shaking hands with the manager, left the office to prepare for the test flight. There were still many unknowns regarding the success of the voyage to Mars, but now he would be to deal with a pilot holding secrets. This felt like a dangerous place to be, should he have a contingency plan? When would the public be informed of the venture if ever? Where there any other secret to be discovered once on their mission? Time would tell and Stephen felt now that he was actually an employee not the employer. This was however the first manned mission to Mars, if it was successful, history would know about it's nuances. The important thing to do was to proceed and document the experience fully.

The first test flight was "textbook". Takeoff at 7:00 am to the second. Climb out was controlled within two knots of airspeed and one degree of pitch angle. Three redundant mission management computers (with two spare backups) initiated guidance to four flight directors which in turn controlled 4 autopilots (only one which was engaged) to the aircraft control surfaces and engine controls. Although manual control was available at any time, the flights were controlled by computers. This was not the case during takeoff and the last moments of landings. With the mission control computers and flight directors, every parameter was optimized for the climb to 50,000 feet. Normally, a 747 would struggle to reach such an altitude, but wing enhancements and engine tweaks allowed this to happen although only with mission control computer authority. At the height of the flight the stall speed and high speed buffet airspeeds where within three knots of each other. Any variation beyond that window would result in uncontrolled flight. No pilot would enjoy flying an aircraft the size of a 747 while it was stalled and out of control.

The crew was so busy monitoring flight systems, communicating and following the test cards that they had no time to think about the dangers of such precise flight requirements. The flight lasted for 1.2 hours and came to a successful end with a smooth landing. Stephen and Benjamin had the advantage of having a multitude of simulated and real flights in 747s before the test flight. The cockpit flow was rehearsed many times over to allow both flight crew members to do their jobs efficiently. The Mission Management Computer (MMC) did a flawless job with the flight and was capable of alerting the crew of upcoming events like changes of attitude or speed. The other MMCs "watched" and would only alert the crew if there was a discrepancy between their computations and the primary MMC. On the ground the computers had been exercised for 1000s of hours and had been tested for catastrophic failures, loss of power etc. It was comforting to see them work in real life however, and finally the whole aircraft could still be flown manually in the event of major computer malfunctions.

The second test flight also went well, which lasted four hours and included complex maneuvers like in-flight refueling procedures and engine out tests. Liquid oxygen was transferred to a holding tank in the fuselage and temperatures monitored through out the cabin to detect problems related to handling the LOX. Again no problems however only about 15% of the total load was actually transferred. Stability proved well within safely limits and the flight again was followed by a smooth landing and considered a success. The test card included 126 separate items, so the crew was understandably tired after the flight. Unfortunately, as will all test flights the de-briefing and report writing followed to make a very full day.

The final test flight would require more LOX and would include a test firing of the rocket engine. The solar cells on the outside fuselage would also be tested including a startup of the ion engines. Before that flight, the other crew members would be briefed and flown in simulators to prepare them for the sensations of flight and flight test, as they would get to experience planned emergency drills while in the air. They also would get to experience the test firing of the rocket engine.

Before the final test flights however Boeing had a few more modifications to do; some were part of the test program results. These included modifying the wing vortex generators and gap seals. This change would further improve the flying characteristics of the aircraft and in addition minimize the incursion of dust once the aircraft landed on the Martian surface. The other changes done to the 747 however were for the satellite launch systems which would fire several "special" satellites out the belly of the aircraft as it went through low earth orbit.

For the final test flights the technicians loaded up 10 dummy masses to test the shock and vibration on the satellites as the rocket engine was ignited and run. The final weight of the 747 for the last test flight would be the same as the real mission flight. This would require careful takeoff procedures followed by a shallow climb angle to be controlled by the MCC. Because of the extra instrumentation included in the flight it could be the most dangerous. Wire bundles and coaxial cable ran through the cockpit and cabin areas impeding movement. The crew in the event of a problem would have a hard time maneuvering about and might not make it to the hatch to bail out. But as with all of the test flights, the crew members practiced every eventuality and became almost automatons during the emergency drills.

On the day of the final test flight, the crew woke up early, ate and donned their flight suits. They again reviewed the status of the aircraft and having memorized their activities began their work in silence. After the equipment was deemed ready, they walked out to the aircraft waiting for them on the tarmac. After climbing aboard, they reviewed the inside of the cabin with the technicians and engineers, checked all safety systems and strapped in for the flight. After verifying that everyone was strapped in and the hatch locked, Stephen worked the pre-start checklist until they were all ready to begin the test flight. The engines were lit and electrical power brought on line. With extensive system tests performed and verified, they taxied onto the runway, fully loaded and after cleared for takeoff, advanced the throttles to 91% to begin their takeoff roll. At first the aircraft seemed to barely move while at the same time vibrating significantly due to the engine thrust. After a few second, speed increased and the vibrations started to smooth out. Speed increased quickly and after 6000 feet of runway was used up, Stephen slowly brought the control column aft to allow the nose wheel to lift off of the runway. The wheel was allowed to come off only about a foot and would remain there as the aircraft increased in speed and became ready to fly. At around 8000 feet the 747 lightened the load on it's main gear and levitated into the air. A shallow pitch angle was established to allow the aircraft to accelerate to its safe climb out speed. The gear was retracted and flaps incrementally brought into the wing until flush with the trailing edge. Although still quite noticeable, the vibrations felt during takeoff were subsiding. At a safe altitude and airspeed, the throttles were retracted to climb power setting and the MCC engaged. Even with the competent hand flying skills of the pilots, the aircraft vibrations again diminished once a faster and more accurate autopilot system was engaged. Now the work would begin by all crew members as they had to complete tasks during all of the next phases of flight. The flight card included a straight out departure and climb to 30,000 feet. This took some coordination with the air traffic controllers in charge of the sector, however because they flew directly West, the flight would soon be out of busy airspace. It took 35 minutes to get to altitude where the flight director smoothly lowered the nose and selected a stable attitude to maintain speed and altitude. Orbiting 20 miles in front of them was a air tanker specially fitted with liquid oxygen. The radar onboard the 747 locked on to the tanker and the MCC commanded the autopilot to turn directly towards the plane. When within one mile of the tanker, the 747 slowed to closure rate and brought the aircraft to within 50 yards of the tanker. At this point the pilots took over and manually flew formation, slowly closing the gap between planes until the boom operator in the tanker could place the fueling probe into the 747 receptacle for the liquid oxygen.

The previous tests with the LOX had proven safe however this time the full load would be transferred. Because of the extreme cold of the LOX, the junction between the probe and receptacle started to form large ice particles. These fell off when the planes moved relative to each however the ice would fly back and come dangerously close to the tail components of the 747. The boom operator noticed this and asked if the 747 crew wanted to stop the refueling operation. After review of the tail via CCD camera, the flight crew decided to continue with the operation. Meanwhile in the back of the cabin, the scientists were noticing an increase in fog and ice buildup around the internal tank. They became concerned because the whole contraption in the rear of the plane was now hissing and blowing fog about. For the first time, the crew sensed the real danger in flying an aircraft soon to be spacecraft into space.   So many things needed to go right and work perfectly. But the best thing for the crew was to do their job, this would minimize any fear generated by the "what if" scenarios.   After a tense five minutes, the loading of LOX was finally complete. The tanker pulled it's fuel probe back as the final chunks of ice flew past the tail. The tanker then banked to the right to allow the 747 room to complete it's climb to 50,000 feet for the rocket test. After another 15 minutes, the aircraft was at altitude and stabilized.   The MCC announced that it was time for the test firing and the crew knew that this meant cinching down their seat belts and shoulder harnesses. After a countdown of 15 seconds, the MCC engaged the turbo pumps to transfer LOX and jet fuel (kerosene) into the rocket chamber for ignition. The engine fired with a loud boom and quickly increased it's output from 0 to 200,000 pounds of thrust pushing the crew members back into their seats. The aircraft started to shake and the reaction control jets started to augment the aerodynamic surfaces to fly the accelerating 747 through the speed of sound and upwards to 80,000 feet where the rocket engine would be shut down. The noise and vibration was significant but the course of the aircraft steady.   The flight to the new altitude took less than 20 seconds at which point the rocket pumps were shut down and venting valves opened to clean the pipes of explosive gases. As a result of the loss of thrust and the arc of the flight path, the crew now found themselves weightless while unattached pencils and notebooks floated around the cabin. This effect would last until the aircraft descended below 50,000 feet where aerodynamic forces would allow the wings to start flying again. This second process took another four minutes to complete. At the bottom of the arc, the MCC slowly brought the nose up to the horizon and gravity again took effect.

From the standpoint of the autopilot and flight directors, everything went normally. From the standpoint of the crew, they just had the roller coaster ride of their lives. Stunned by the excitement after the level off, the crew took a few moments to compose themselves and return to work. The rest of the test card was definitely boring compared to the 0g portion of the test flight. A multitude of tests were completed and the aircraft banked back to the direction of the runway in Everett. During the return flight, the ion engines embedded into the trailing edges of the wings were started up; due to the atmospheric pressure the amount of thrust was minor but measurable; enough to verify the thrust equations and extrapolate the performance when in the vacuum of space. The descent was un-eventful as was the approach to landing. Another smooth touchdown followed and the crew sat for several minutes contemplating their experience.

"Well, that was interesting," said Judy.

"No kidding," answered Nanci. "Although I knew was going to happen, I was not prepared for the sensation of weightlessness." The crew secured the aircraft systems, shut down everything and un-buckled. Once up they made their way to the hatch to meet the technicians and de-plane. Tired, they then walked into the hangar and made their way to the de-briefing room to meet several engineers and scientists interested in the data from their flight as well as the crew's reflections on the experience. This de-briefing had a twist this time however, the psychologists were present and the focus on the flight was actually a final evaluation of the crews ability to handle the new sensations of weightlessness and still carry out complex procedures.

"I noticed a time gap between the initiation of the 0 g maneuver and your completing the check list item 87, Judy, can you enlighten us as to why you were day dreaming," asked Dr. Knox the head psychologist for the mission.

"I was not prepared for the sensation of floating around in my seat so it took a few seconds to re orient myself and get back to task, sorry," answered Judy.

Quickly Dr. Knox retorted, "During a real space flight, when conditions change you don't have any time to hesitate, your mind wanderings could cause major problems in the event of an emergency, you just can't screw up like that. To quote a famous movie actor, failure is not an option, do you understand?"

"I do, it won't happen again, doctor," answered Judy sheepishly.

"It had better not, in fact all of you crew member had some measurable amount of hesitation during that phase, we can't have that, stick to your tasks, does everyone understand how important it is?" asked the doctor. All crew member nodded in compliance. No time for fun until the pressure is off, which would be well after launch. For the next four hours, the flight tapes were reviewed, the crew interviewed and reports written.

In actuality, Stephen thought, the crew acted like the MDRS crew in Utah, focused on task, but human enough to look out of the window every once in a while. That would be just fine on the real flight.

Chapter 8:   No time like the present

"We are in the groove, all systems nominal and what a view"

It is one thing to practice, simulate and imagine the feeling of flying in space, but as all astronauts and cosmonauts will tell you, once you are really there, it is truly wondrous.   No one ever forgets the experience and in fact decades after a flight, these people can relate stories about their space work with clarity.   When the human mind

103

witnesses something amazing or traumatic, a part of the brain is reserved to accurately record fine details surrounding the event. Many years later, one can remember what was said, the color of the sky, if it was windy and many other facts to paint a very complete picture of such an experience. This part of the brain must really have been made for the exposure to space flight. Clearly human beings in their pioneering inclinations savor the effects of lighting up this part of the mind. If there is a hard thing to do or a unique place to visit, those with the most active sensation recording centers are the first to try. This was an accurate description of the original MDRS crew as well as the flight crew. Driven, unable to reflect until the work is finished.

A date was set for the real flight. Bugs were worked out in the aircraft systems, mechanical details were attended to, software was enhanced. The final days before the flight were consumed with discussions of safety procedures by the whole crew and flight operations in other 747s and fighter jets for the cockpit crew. Although busy until late at night, the flight crew as well as the ground support personnel knew that they would be full of energy once the launch day arrived. It was not easy to sleep for anyone as the final days passed. Stephen knew however that it was important to rest, so the day before the launch he went home early, drank a beer and starred out the window of his home trying to remember the images of the plants, grass and birds he would not see for a long time. Professionally speaking, this would not be a big deal, from the human perspective however, leaving earth behind *is* a big deal. The earth becomes inaccessible, you don't just go home when you feel like it. Communications are delayed at the great distance of Mars, bandwidth is limited and getting video of the family or even mission control is an exercise in patience. He would miss this place as would the others, but that pioneer part of the brain was too powerful to ignore. The great journey beckoned and it was his job to fly the mission.

The other crew members curiously had the same kind of feelings that Stephen had. Miss this place, sure, but go on the mission.....absolutely. No time like the present. Nothing like making history.

The morning was clear and calm, by the time the crew members arrived to "work" the place was crowded with technicians and engineers and of course the men in black suits with sunglasses on. During the pre-flight, every nut, bolt and rivet was examined thoroughly, every container filled, every tank topped off. The wings hung low with their loads, the aircraft was shouldered with a great burden, it would be lifted off soon enough as it would be in zero or one g for most of the rest of its life. Special ablative paints had been added to the underside of the craft with extra coatings on the nose and leading edges of both the wings and empenage. These would allow the autopilot to fly the aircraft back into the earth's atmosphere, using temperature as pitch control. Basically, it meant that as the 747 entered the atmosphere, it would do so only at a very shallow angle, skipping off the upper layers until speed was gradually reduced. Then, steeper and steeper angles of descent could be used to find "real" air at about 50,000 feet. Until then, the attitude of the aircraft would be controlled by thruster jets.

As a backup, it had been decided that if it could not re-enter the earth's atmosphere without damage due to the Mars landing, the return trip would be to the International Space Station (where Leah was the Medical Director). They would rendezvous there and transfer themselves and the geological samples to the station, whereupon the Space Shuttle would take them home. The Shuttle had again gone through refurbishment after a second fatal accident. It had flown many more safe missions and due for a replacement in several more years. Interestingly, the 747 might be the first semi-replacement (not including the Soyuz spacecraft). This was an aircraft that was first flown in the late 1960's and according to some aerospace engineers, had more sophisticated avionics than the Apollo spacecraft of the same era. Unlike the Apollo, it had been extensively upgraded and now found itself ready to embark on a space voyage.

The air/space craft was pulled out of the hangar and stood ready for the crew. They had all suited up and had the standard breakfast meal. All of the rituals of special sweaters and incantations were present. The crew would take many of the support personnel up with them in spirit. As with all spacecraft, the people who worked on it share a special pride of having "their fingerprints on it." The air was thick with anticipation. It was now time to say goodbye.

The flight crew climbed up the air stairs to the hatch. Before they entered they each turned around to wave and say goodbye. The ground crew gathered around the stairs to wave back, all of them knew that this would be a momentous journey, and if successful, historic. We went to the Moon in 1969, then to Mars on this date.

The hatch was sealed and the crew members without talking, took their seats and strapped in. The craft looked stuffed with provisions and scientific equipment. The tanks full, the weight at max, nothing more could be added.

Stephen picked up the checklist and started from the top.

"Departure briefing... Complete."

107

"FMCs, radios... Programmed, set and verified."

"ADIRS... Nav, aligned."

"Fuel panel... Pumps on, cross feed closed."

"Cabin status panels... On."

"Oxygen check... Complete."

"Engine Master Switches... Off."

"Parking brake... Set, pressure normal."

"Altimeters... 30.12 set."

"Airspeed bugs... 866,000 pounds, flaps 20, V1 160 knots, VR 165, V2 168."

"Doors and windows... Closed and locked."

"Cabin preparation... Complete, all green lights."

"Control Check... Complete."

"Engine anti-ice... Off."

"Auto brakes... Max."

"Flaps... 20 degrees, set, detent."

"Engine mode selector... Normal/Ignition start."

"ECAM status check... Complete."

"Crew member checks... Complete."

"Transponder... Traffic."

"Takeoff memo... Green."

With all engines started, they advanced the throttles to 40% initially to get the bird rolling then back to 15% to continue a steady pace. Each crew member was busy checking and re-checking all of the systems, just like the previous test flights. The control tower gave them the clearance for a straight out departure to 8,000 feet then left turn to a heading of 170 for the six hour flight to the equator. The 747 would proceed to a specified GPS point and meet up with two tankers for airborne refueling operations. The first tanker would load more jet fuel for the rocket burn, the second would then load the liquid oxygen. Minutes later, they would light the rocket engine and burn it for eight minutes, this would increase their velocity to 17,000 miles per hour and place them in low earth orbit. As the 747 rumbled out to the runway, the crew members could see a crowd of people in the control tower cab and crowds of people on the tarmac, most of them with white shirts and ties (paying respect for the engineers that designed the early NASA spacecraft). Some waved but most did not, as it looked like any other aircraft departure except for the rocket engine bolted onto the tail of the aircraft. As the 747 bumped over the concrete pads on the way to the takeoff point, the crew settled in and were happy about finally starting their voyage. Judy smiled a bit as she and the rest of the crew were very satisfied to get going.   Given priority, the 747 lumbered past several other waiting jets whose crew member waved and said "good luck" and "God speed" over the radio.

Mars Life

The aircraft taxied to the beginning of the runway just over the numbers and stopped.

Final checks were completed, the tower reported, "Boeing Zero Zero Seven Romeo Zebra, cleared for takeoff, maintain runway heading, climb to 8,000."

"Roger, Zero Zero Seven Romeo Zebra is cleared for takeoff, straight out to 8,000, see ya."

"Romeo Zebra, affirmative, have a good flight." With that, Stephen advanced the throttles to 91% N1 and again the bird slowly started rolling. Again at 6,000 feet down the runway the control column was pulled back gently to unload the nose wheel, and again the fully loaded 747 levitated off of the main gear and rose into the air.

"Gear up," said the commander.

"Gear up and stowed," reported the first officer.

"Flaps up," continued the commander, at the appropriate speed.

"Flaps coming up, slats in, spoilers off," returned the first officer. "Zero Zero Seven Romeo Zebra contact departure, good day." radioed the tower. The commander keyed the radio mike button.

"Going to departure, good day."

"Departure control, Boeing Zero Zero Seven Romeo Zebra heavy with you through 2,000 for eight."

"Zero Zero Seven Romeo Zebra heavy, departure

control, radar contact, left turn on course, climb and maintain Flight Level two zero zero, no speed restrictions."

"Zero Zero Seven Romeo Zebra heavy, left turn one seven zero and out of 3,000 for flight level two zero zero, no speed restrictions."

"Zero Zero Seven Romeo Zebra traffic one o'clock five miles a Cessna, do you have him in sight?"

" Zero Zero Seven Romeo Zebra looking, no joy."

"And Romeo Zebra, you will be joined by a flight of six F-15s approaching from your eight o'clock position, they have you on radar."

"Romeo Zebra roger."

The flight crew had not expected this, but it was welcome in the sense that all other traffic would be diverted to allow them the most efficient speed and climb profiles. Because air traffic control had lifted the speed restrictions, they did not need to slow down to 250 knots below 10,000 feet. They in fact were passing 9,000 feet with an airspeed of 320 knots and climbing. Stephen looked to his right and saw the first officer watching the systems and primary flight displays with intensity. Stephen smiled and keyed the mike button.

"Departure control, this if Romeo Zebra, we still don't have that Cessna."

Mars Life

At that moment, a CFI flying over the ocean with a new student said, "Did you hear that?"

"No," replied the student, not used to aviation radio conversations.

"My plane," the CFI said, and as instructed, the student released the controls and removed his feet from the rudder pedals instantly. The CFI had drilled into all of his students that the controls would instantly heat up to incandescent temperatures when he said those magic words. The moment the student released the controls the instructor pulled the power level to idle, pushed full right rudder, cranked full left aileron, pointed the nose at the ground and dove the plane for its life. Flying sideways, the Cessna was more of a brick than an airplane and descended rapidly to avoid a collision. Minus two g's were felt sideways in the cockpit.

"Learned this in 'Nam," the instructor spoke quietly, and after 10 very long seconds said, "Your plane". He released the pressure on the controls and again they were level, quiet and humming along.   The   student, somewhat glad to be alive, looked at the CFI, who was looking bored and checking his watch, took the controls and considered seriously changing his shorts upon landing.

****

"Roger Romeo Zebra, he is now at your 6 o'clock closing at minus 280 knots, descending 3,500 feet per minute, no factor at this time will advise if there is a change."

"Romeo Zebra thank you," Stephen looked at the first officer who had now stopped staring at the displays and was looking at the commander.

"And who says air traffic controllers don't have a sense of humor," said the commander smiling. The first officer smiled and sat back in his seat a bit more relaxed.

What they did not realize was that the 747 had passed over the Cessna at about 100 feet and 340 knots.

"Romeo Zebra, contact Los Angeles Center on one three four point six five."

"Romeo Zebras going to thirty four sixty five, good day."

After the frequency change, the commander radioed again.

"Los Angeles Center, Zero Zero Seven Romeo Zebra heavy is with you through 12,000 for flight level two zero zero."

"Zero Zero Seven Romeo Zebra, radar contact, climb to flight level 350."

"Up to three five zero, Romeo Zebra."

Another voice:

"Los Angeles Center, Mad Dog five zero with you, flight of six joining up with Romeo Zebra."

"Mad Dog five zero, roger, Romeo Zebra is cleared to flight level three five zero."

"Three five roger."

With this, the 747 crew looked out the windows and soon saw the six F-15s joining in formation around the Boeing. They flew tight and precisely in a V formation with the 747 at point. It would be their duty to make sure that the 747 got to it's final altitude (as a plane) of 50,000 feet without any "interruptions". The flight of six F-15s would be replaced every two hours with a new group during the rest of the flight to the equator.

After 22 minutes the 747 leveled off at it's assigned altitude.

"Center, Romeo Zebra is level at three five zero."

"Romeo Zebra, L A Center thank you. Contact Fish Eye one on one two seven point two five."

"Romeo Zebras going to two seven two five, good day."

"Good day and good luck."

With that the 747 crew switched over to the new frequency and would now talk to an AWACS aircraft that would follow them down to the equator and coordinate the other aircraft that would be working with the 747. Romeo Zebra would now change their call sign to Thales one for the rest of their mission. Thales was the first philosopher and was also credited with discovering static electricity which eventually resulted in the discovery of electro-magnetism, the fundamental force behind the new ion engine built into the wings of the 747. As a pre-Socratic philosopher, he taught that everything in the universe had a relationship with water. It was from this that life sprang and with which life could only continue. The Thales 1 crew was flying to Mars in search of water, for this held the key in colonizing the planet with life. It had been long thought that due to the land formations on Mars, water must have existed long ago and ran in rivers and streams toward lakes and oceans. The hope was that water was still abundant on Mars albeit under the ground or in cliff sides. The commander checked in.

"Fish Eye this is Thales one with you level at three five zero."

"Thales one this is Fish Eye, good morning, the traffic has been cleared ahead and the weather looks good."

"Thank you Fish Eye, any sign of that Cessna following us?"

"Negative Thales one, the bogey has bugged out!"

Again the Thales flight crew smiled and could relax

for a while until they met up with the tankers. The flight was very smooth, a good omen. The equipment was working flawlessly giving the crew confidence for the upcoming challenge of orbital insertion.

Stephen looked at Benjamin, "your plane" and unbuckled to go back to check the scientists and stretch a bit. Benjamin was a bit wide eyed sitting in the cockpit alone with six F-15s within ten feet of the wings and behind him a complete spacecraft with astronauts in orange suits. It didn't seem to NASA that it was very professional for the commander to just get up to wander around but this was an unusual mission considering the commander owned the plane and the government owned everything else. He also thought about his real mission, to launch several "birds" for the launch customer, no matter what, that had to happen.

Stephen went back to the crew quarters where Nanci and Judy were talking and monitoring instruments.

"How is everyone doing?" asked Stephen.

"Just fine, everything is in order, how far are we from the equator now?" asked Judy.

"We are about three hours away now and everything is going smoothly up in the front office," replied the commander.

"If you go to channel three on the aircraft monitor system, it will show you the navigational track and the positions of the orbital insertion initial fix. The visitors outside will be with us until we reach the equator and climb up to 50,000 feet. We are also being tracked by an AWACS and who knows who else, continued the commander. Go ahead and have something to eat, I am going to get some coffee for me and Benjamin and we will eat later."

With that, Stephen made his way back into the aircraft to check out the various pieces of equipment and in particular the rocket fuel tanks that would soon be filled with liquid oxygen. On his return he stopped and poured some coffee for himself and the first officer. It felt good to be flying and better to be on a great mission. He passed the scientists as he walked forward and saw that they had loosened their belts and were rummaging for food.

"No little crackers on this flight," said Nanci. "When do we see the movie?"

Stephen replied, "In about four hours, I will let you know." He smiled and continued up into the cockpit where Benjamin was pleasantly surprised to see coffee. Stephen then sat down and belted in, handing the cup to Benjamin.

"How is it going up here?" he asked.

"Well the lead F-15 pilot, Mad Dog, saw you leave and became concerned, I told him that you went back to use the flight phone to call your wife and tell her you left the stove on," said Benjamin.

117

"Very funny Benj, you're a real crack up," replied Stephen.

The flight went on for several more hours, mainly uneventful and basically in a straight line which in itself is boring. The Mad Dog six was replaced with the Cougar six then the Raven six. The AWACS changed once due to the fact that the 747 was a bit faster than them, they now were talking to Eye Ball two.

"Where do they get these names?" asked Benjamin.

"From too much TV, they're all a bunch of scope dopes," replied Stephen.

"However we are now approaching the initial approach fix for tanker one, it's time to get back to work," Stephen announced over the crew intercom.

The crew members started to focus again as it was getting close to orbital insertion time. The next few hours would be critical and performance had to be at it's best.

"Thales one this is Raven flight leader."

"Raven flight leader, Thales, go ahead."

"We have the tankers on radar now and you need to slow to Mach point seven and descend to flight level 280."

"Thales one slowing to point seven and descending to flight level two eight zero."

With that, Benjamin reached over and set the auto-

118

throttles to Mach point seven and the altitude bug to 28,000. The big 747 started to slow down and descend. The four throttle controls moved back in unison to about 30% N1 and the nose lowered pitch to maintain the airspeed set into the autopilot. The F-15s did the same in formation. They had to descend through two cloud layers on their way down and Stephen noticed that even in the soup, the F-15s were still in tight formation.

"Impressive," he thought, "but you are not yet a jet eye yet." Concerned about his mind wandering, Stephen got back to work. "Coming up on 28,000," announced Stephen. "Lets all cinch up and do this right."

At 28,000 feet the nose slowly pitch up, the throttle controls worked their way forward and the altimeters settled exactly on 28,000 feet. About five miles ahead the tanker was waiting. The Thales crept forward mindful not to run over the waiting tanker. At one mile, Stephen pushed the auto throttle disconnect button in the control column while Benjamin silenced the alarm. Stephen started to manipulate the throttle controls and maneuver the aircraft carefully underneath the tanker to allow the boom operator to connect to the fuel receptacle on the nose of the 747. At the point of contact, Benjamin announced that the valves were open. Jet fuel started flowing into the almost dry tanks. They would not take on a full load from this tanker however, so only four wing tanks were filled. This took about 15 minutes of precise hand flying. After Benjamin announced that the tanks were full, the boom operator backed off and retracted . Soon the tanker climbed away and turned to the West to return to it's base. Stephen placed the 747 back on autopilot, and could now relax for a bit. He would now assist Benjamin in the next in flight refueling, which would happen in less than 10 minutes.

Nine minutes later, right on schedule was the LOX tanker. Benjamin switched the distribution valves to now fill the internal LOX tanks and switched off the auto pilot to hand fly another approach to the tanker. This transfer went as well as the first leaving Thales full of fuel and ready for an orbital insertion burn. The second tanker retracted it's boom and banked to the right leaving the fully loaded 747 flying due east along the equator. Doing this would allow the greatest amount of earth's help in reaching orbit. This in turn would minimize fuel use and allow greater payload. Even so, everything had to be perfect and there would be few chances of getting out of trouble in the case of an emergency. The crew went over the final earthbound checklists and manually inspected the plumbing in the back of the cabin, which by now was creaking and groaning under the chill of liquid oxygen. The wings too were frosting up in spots, showing where the other tanks of LOX were. The pilots knew that they would have to start the rocket burn soon, lest the aircraft become unstable due to loss of laminar flow across the wings. The aircraft then climbed to 50,000 feet, set speed at Mach .94 and the crew donned their helmets.

The commander started the final check list:

"Pre Orbital Burn checklist ready?"

"Ready."

"Burn Control Computer self check complete?"

"Check."

"Autopilot set to Orbital Insertion?"

"Check."

"Propellant valves open."

"Check."

"Vent valves closed."

"Vent valves closed and pressure check valves operational."

"Nozzle actuators on line."

"Nozzle actuators on line and tested good."

"Igniters on?."

"Igniter on."

"Turbo pumps engage."

"Turbo pumps engaged and pressures nominal, we have a clean start."

With that the crew felt the g forces building up and

the noise increasing. At the point of maximum aerodynamic stress, the nose pitched up to a 40 degree climb angle, the reaction control jets were firing and the nozzle vectoring actuators were moving about to allow for the smoothest ride possible, which really wasn't that smooth. The craft shook and swayed as the g forces continued to build. The crew felt as if they were in a centrifuge lying on their backs as their body weight increased to many times it's normal earth bound weight. Judy looked outside briefly and found that the horizon was getting a definite arc to it and the sky was turning darker and darker. Moving her head sideways under these conditions caused her to feel a bit dizzy so she averted the window gazing and looked forward. The pilots up front were busy monitoring pressure gages and the attitude indicators. The profile looked nominal as the computers were doing their job. Impressive considering the vibration levels. After a very long eight minutes, the fuel was spent and after the rocket ceased running the silence was deafening. The craft arced over to be parallel to the earth's surface. The turbo pumps whined down as they were no longer needed and the plumbing again creaked due to the fact that they could return to normal temperatures. Also, at the moment of propellant exhaustion, the crew went from plus three g's to weightlessness in about two seconds. The sensation was amazing as all that weight quickly lifted off the crew members and continued to be lifted until they became fully weightless. For some reason, every crew member smiled at this point. The big 747 was now 160 miles above the earth's surface and traveling in excess of 17,000 miles per hour, all without the sensation of great speed or being at great altitude. It felt as though they were a space borne object near another larger space borne object, dancing among the stars in the most elegant ballet imaginable. One where position and time where relative. The cockpit crew was still busy going through a post burn checklist making sure that the rocket engine and left over propellants were secure or expelled as the case may be. Having residual flammable vapors floating about near a hot engine bell would not be a good thing, so the bell was purged and cooled with a little bit of remaining LOX. Valves were secured and pressures were monitored for several minutes. It would not be safe until the various engine components cooled down to ambient temperatures.

As the cockpit crew monitored the systems and gages, Judy and Nanci unbuckled and introduced themselves to weightlessness. "Wow, this is very cool," announced Nanci.

"Absolutely amazing," replied Judy, "just beautiful."

Now that the rocket system was becoming safe, Stephen under his agreement with Boeing, turned over the control of activities to Benjamin. His job was to launch several special satellites into earth orbit at very specific positions and intervals. The fact that the bird made it to orbit would save Boeing many millions of dollars and in fact more than pay for the work done on the aircraft including the installation of the rocket engine. The risk was assumed totally by the company however, and both management and workers were cheering the successful launch, but maybe for different reasons. Stephen switched the com system to "orbital."

"Thales one to ground how to you copy?" queried Stephen.

"Thales one this is ground we copy you five by five and are receiving good telemetry. How was the ride?"

"Ride was pretty smooth, engine performed perfectly and is now secured."

"Great, your orbit looks just about perfect, switch to echo one," (echo one was a secure channel).

"Going to echo one."

"Ground this is Thales on echo one how do you copy."

"Thales this is ground you are five by five, coming up on point alpha, confirm computer alignment."

"Roger, computer alignment confirmed, birds one and two in green mode and ready for launch."

"Roger that, Thales."

A few minutes later, two spherical satellites simultaneously were ejected from the port and starboard sides of the fuselage, this would minimize any attitude correction necessary for the (now) spacecraft.

"Thales, ground control confirms a good launch reset computers for point beta."

"Ground this is Thales, computers reset to point beta and armed."

12 minutes later, another set of spherical satellites were ejected, followed another 15 minutes later with the last set of satellites meant for earth orbit.

"Thales this is ground control, we confirm launch of all satellites, you may secure launch doors."

"Launch doors secured and pressurized, we confirm good launches."

With that simple exercise, the Thales crew had paid their way to space. There was still one more satellite in the launch bay, but this would not be used until they reached Mars. For now the crew continued with the orbital insertion checklist.

"OK, launch bay pressurization check."

"Pressurization complete and checked."

"Fuel cell 1 start."

"Fuel cell 1 started and on line."

"Fuel cell 2 start."

"Fuel cell 2 started and on line."

"Main bus A check."

"Main bus A checked and all voltages nominal."

"Main bus B check."

"Main bus B checked and all voltages nominal."

"Emergency bus check."

"Emergency bus checked and all voltages nominal."

"Cabin pressurization check."

"Pressure nominal, no leaks and all out gas valves in closed position."

"Deploy solar cell arrays."

"Deployment sequence initiated.........arrays extended and locked, doors closed."

"Array voltage check."

"Array voltage nominal."

"Ok lets go to the ion engine startup checklist."

"Roger."

"Close ion engine main breaker."

"Ion main breaker closed and flight computer verifies ion engine system on line."

"Ion engine pre test sequence initiate."

"Ion engine pre test sequence initiated and calibrating."

"Ion engine control switches to 'startup'."

"Ion engine control switches to 'startup' and all lights green."

"Ion engine control switches to 'run'."

"Ion engine control switches to 'run' position, thrust coming up and all lights green, flight control computer confirms thrust, mission control computer verifies positive control."

With that the engine conceived in a round hab in the middle of Utah by a group of creative scientists began it's operation with a mild sensation of thrust, about .2 g. this level would continue for about a day and a half where the spacecraft would then be able to depart earth's gravitational pull and begin the journey to Mars. Looking out the rear windows of Thales revealed a plasma glowing deep blue emanating from six places near the trailing edge of each wing. The plasma formed an elongated tear drop that trailed 50 feet behind each engine. The primary source of power for the engines were the solar cells along the fuselage augmented by those on the solar panels spread above the spacecraft. The thrust was smooth and controllable without any noise or vibration. The spacecraft was quiet now save for the air re-circulation fans and the crews conversations. The cockpit crew finished up the checklists and allowed the spacecraft mission computers to run all systems.

Mars Life

"Check list complete my side," said the commander.

"Yeah, I am done as well," replied the pilot.

"This is definitely the best seat in the house, look at that beautiful earth. I can see a lightning storm over Africa and the Aurora Borealis, what a sight!"

Even though the crew was now able to unbuckle and leave the cockpit, they waited and looked out the large windows of the 747 at the astounding view of the earth below. In fact, by this time all of the crew members were just looking out the windows in wonderment and in silence. Somehow being in space was a natural thing for these human beings to do. Not that they were special, but maybe just lucky. Again inwardly or visibly they all smiled.

"What's for lunch," asked Stephen as he unbuckled himself and floated slowly back to the main cabin.

"Well there's not much left," replied Nanci, pointing to the storage bins jammed with 2 years of food.

"Ok, I will just rummage around here and find something, maybe some left overs," replied Stephen.

He floated back to the middle of the spacecraft where bins and lockers held all of the food and other human essentials. Below in the belly cargo areas were more food stuffs and other essentials. Almost every cubic inch of the spacecraft held something, even the spare areas in the wings and tail. The only really open spot was about amidships where there was a common area roughly 20 feet wide and 35 feet long. This area was surrounded by flat screens and computer equipment but served as a comfortable place to eat and relax. In this area could be found movies, music and games. There was a central circular table in the middle for eating or playing cards. Much thought was put into the layout of the spacecraft considering how long the crew would be aboard. There were individual private staterooms (about the size as those at the MDRS station) and two bathroom areas complete with showers. Down the center of the cabin was a two foot wide walkway, with electromagnets embedded in it. This was installed to allow the crew members to use shoes with magnets in them if they chose. The bathrooms were also equipped with this feature. About 2/3 s the way back from the nose of the spacecraft was a circular centrifuge. It also spanned the 20 feet of the fuselage and was a complete circular race track that was motorized. If a crew member needed a one g environment, he or she would go into this area, shut the doors fore and aft, and switch on the electric motors to start the unit spinning. When inside the sensation of being on earth or Mars could be felt by adjusting the spin rate and up to two members could sit inside. This would be the area were most exercise could be done and where the adjustment to the various gravitational fields would be accomplished. Because of the anti-torque required for the rest of the spacecraft, a small ion thruster was placed on one wingtip and would be activated once the centrifuge was turned on. Considering the great size of the spacecraft it could seem very roomy which would be important for crew comfort.

Chapter Nine: The Six week vacation

"We are at the initial approach fix, prepare for landing"

For the first 24 hours the crew spent most of it's time acclimating to the micro-g environment. That meant that half of them became ill for the initial part of the voyage. The stomach needs to get used to floating about, and because the bodily fluids spread evenly the sensation of thirst is nonexistent so the astronauts had to remember to hydrate themselves periodically. Medical tests were performed several times and all personnel wore a medical harness that telemetered the data to the cabin computer system for monitoring.

Before the flight to Mars was to begin however they

had to break orbit and re-orient the spacecraft. The speed had increased steadily over the past day to allow their orbit to climb to beyond 300 miles altitude. Within another 12 hours this would increase another 200 miles and by adjusting their pitch angle accordingly they would slowly break out of orbit and head toward a spot that Mars would be in a month and a half hence. For safety purposes, the crew strapped in and performed check lists to make sure all systems were working properly. As the moment of pitch change came, Stephen allowed the mission computer to fire the RCS thrusters and slowly the great craft turned to face a new direction, not parallel with the earth's surface anymore. The ion rockets continued to run and after several more hours they noticed that the earth began to grow smaller and smaller. It was almost imperceptible at first, but the fiducial markings on the aft facing TV camera showed a definite shrinking. Their velocity was now approaching 30,000 Miles per hour and would continue to increase until about the mid point between planets, where the ship would be turned 180 degrees to start a slow deceleration.

For now however it was time to get used to monitoring ship's systems and dealing with boredom. And again, like the crew of the MDRS station, these like minded people began a comfortable routine of writing reports on science experiments, e-mailing friends, family and mission control. The diurnal cycle of the spacecraft would slowly change from a 24 hour day to a 24 hour 39.5 minute day over the course of the flight, this would accommodate the Martian day. This was programmed into the computer which kept a mission clock on UTC and a crew clock that varied.

A typical day began with a wake up call, breakfast, a meeting on activities, and the start of "chores." After the basic science or housekeeping "chores" were complete, the crew would either exercise or eat lunch, whichever fell in the rotation. After this period, basic medical testing took place, scientific experiments were continued and finally report writing would take place. Later, dinner would be served followed by a shower (for whoever was in the rotation). Free time would then follow which considering the makeup of this crew, included more science, studying and sometimes a movie. The radio link to the earth was uses to uplink movies and e-mails and the Internet; the downlink would include the e-mails and reports and of course telemetric data about the health of the crew and ship.

The routine became comfortable and the crew got along very well. Although there were times of stress where the spacecraft needed some attention due to a jammed computer or a malfunctioning oven, in general the problems were taken take of with the help of all and as a consequence the crew started to become friends. After two weeks, everyone was acclimated to space life and was having a good time. After three weeks the crew was in countdown mode for the landing. The ship was turned about to start the slow deceleration to Mars. The planet could be plainly seen out of the aft cameras, it grew larger every day and slowly filled the monitors as the spacecraft closed in on orbital insertion. Again the fiducial marks showed the progress of the flight and the crew members would measure the diameter almost every day to see their progress.

After the mid-course maneuver was complete the radar system was turned on and at once found the planet. There were about six radar systems on board the Thales. The first to run was a low frequency system that also could be used as a short wave transceivers. Periodically, this radio portion was used to contact Ham radio operators on earth for some interesting "QSOs". These conversations were always friendly but every once in a while the operator on the other end thought it was a ruse. After a fashion, a frequency was chosen that would be monitored and every evening at 8:00 MST the Thales would be on the air and talk to whoever was interested. After a few weeks there would be at least a dozen operators waiting to contact the Thales and ask about space travel. Many elementary schools had ham operators who brought in tapes of conversations or arranged to have a radio present during an evening so the kids could talk to the astronauts. The adults would typically ask technical questions or "what's it like" questions whereas the kids usually asked questions about going outside or what they ate or if it was cold. The Thales crew enjoyed this part of the day, especially if kids were on the other end. In several cases the radio operators on earth would patch in a telephone call to a crew members family or friends, so it was more like a telephone call. The biggest problem of course was, as Thales grew farther and farther away, the time delay became so long that conversations had to take place using typed modulation techniques like packet radio. Also, propagation became a variable with some evenings having crystal clear conversations and others being filled with noise. On average the higher the frequency of operation the better. In fact, a few times the Thales crew actually talked to operators on hand held radios out in fields or in their cars. This happened only on the first part of the journey, later more sophisticated equipment was required by the earth bound amateur radio operators.

The crew was definitely having fun even with a reasonable work load. Times were good for them, they all felt proud of their mission and took care to do the best possible work, even if it required doing something out of their particular experience. Nanci would help with calibrating radar equipment, Benjamin would help out with the plant cultures and other biological tasks. Stephen and Judy also traded tasks;   this reminded Stephen of his experience back in Utah with the MDRS crew and he again felt that that crew could have easily been a part of this flight.

But on one particular evening, Nanci and Benjamin were working in the plant and seed storage section of the spacecraft. This was an area of some 20 feet by 10 feet alongside the sunlit side of the fuselage. All the windows were uncovered and usually had a beautiful view of the stars and sun. (You can see both at the same time in space). It was usually warm from the incoming sunlight and various crew members would sometimes go here and read or otherwise relax. On this particular night, Benjamin was helping Nanci take swab samples of various areas in the spacecraft and plant storage area to check for microbial growth. They would swab a surface or air vent and take the swabs back to the plant storage area where they would wipe the swabs in an auger dish. These dishes were about three inches in diameter, ½ inch tall and made of plastic or glass. Inside was a growing medium, auger which would feed the microbes that were collected by the swabs and let them grow enough to be examined and categorized. After the dishes were prepared they were put in a warm oven to accelerate the process, which would take a day or two.

Benjamin found that he liked to work with Nanci, partly for learning new things and partly because he was drawn to her pleasant personality. She was disarming and intelligent and they could easily talk about any subject. Often they would inadvertently talk about things beyond a particular prearranged time where other activities had been planned. Stephen and Judy came to notice this fact and it's implications, but Stephen was married and Judy was very close to someone back home. Nanci and Benjamin however were single, and the interactions were different as a result. This night was particularly beautiful with Orion in full glory and the sun providing a warming light and the faint hint of a comet about to round the sun with a tail many millions of miles long. It caused the two workers to pause and look out the windows.

"We are so lucky to be here," said Nanci.

"You're absolutely right about that, it's amazing."

After another moment, they turned around to continue to work and inadvertently Benjamin placed his hand on Nanci's, which was sitting on a lab bench. Ordinarily, this would have evoked an "oh excuse me" or a "sorry," but it didn't; they both jumped a bit as if having been mildly shocked. Benjamin, ever the perfect worded rhetorician... said nothing. This began the awkward silence, and Nanci perpetuated the silence by saying, "Oh...I....uh."

A few moments later they both tried to get back to work but the damage had been done. This four second space in time would forever change their lives.

Now as anyone who has had an emotional relationship will attest, every moment after such an encounter is incredibly important. Time becomes a variable not a constant, and as any fiercely attracted couples will tell you, time away from the other is made too long, where time with the other is too short. No one knows why this is true, but it is. The conversations are careful and many times over thought as well, as each member is not sure about the other's feeling quite yet, and does not want to go too slow or too fast in creating the new chemistry. Benjamin's and Nanci's temporal ebbs and flows were now beginning, for there was something natural about all this.

Meanwhile the other crew continued their activities but after a few days, it became obvious to all that something was different. Benjamin and Nanci spent a little more time together and would get a little closer to each other than normal. For now that was ok, however the commander was starting to get worried about loss of concentration upon landing and other critical procedures. There would come a time for "the conversation". No one minded the activities, unless there was a safety issue, in that case everyone was concerned.

The commander started it off, "Looks like you and Nanci are getting along well," initiated Stephen when he and Benjamin were alone in the cockpit one day.

"Oh, yeah, it's really great, she is a wonderful person," replied Benjamin.

"Well, although Judy and I don't mind the relationship, we and especially I am concerned you two will start daydreaming at the wrong time, do you know what I mean," said Stephen.

"Yeah I know, we will be careful I promise, mind if I go back now?" asked Benjamin.

"Not quite yet, do not for a moment forget your duties and work, we are on a mission here, one that you waited a life time to get, don't screw this up or I am going to be all over you and Nanci. Keep your personal activities away from our job here, and if I need you, respond immediately, do you understand?" asked the commander.

"Absolutely," responded Benjamin, "We won't jeopardize the mission."

"Ok, get back to it then," said the commander with a stern look to bring the point home. Benjamin unbuckled and went back to the cabin, cognizant that eyes were on him and Nanci, cognizant also that he really needed to concentrate. There would be plenty of time for play.

Several more days went by and the crew was

getting the feeling that the landing was fast approaching. Many chores needed performing, aligning the navigation system precisely was the most important. During the first part of the mission gross alignments on the order of a few degrees were fine, but as the mission progressed, smaller and more precise adjustments to their flight path were performed. The results of this ever increasing flight precision was that the spacecraft would burn the minimum fuel for a precise entry into the final approach corridor. Days away from the landing, the mission computers started showing tunnel grid displays on the navigation displays. These were rectangles that appeared suspended in space that showed the optimum windows for entry into the final approach glide path. A line tracing the path of the vehicle ran through these windows to show the offsets from a perfect trajectory. Although close, the spacecraft still made minute adjustments every few hours to get even closer to the center point.

Another major task was to attach the landing skids onto the fuselage. Obviously the landing gear would be of no use without a hard runway, they in fact would remain retracted during the landing an trip back and used only if an earth landing was possible. An EVA was necessary to assemble the skids and attach them to pre existing attach points. The components for the skids were stored in the belly portion of the spacecraft. This needed to be de-pressurized before the space suited astronauts could remove the parts to assemble the skids. Benjamin and Judy had trained in a neutral buoyancy tank at NASA for this EVA for hundreds of hours and were certainly ready for the task. Stephen would remain suited up in the cockpit to monitor their progress and Nanci would monitor pressurization systems in the main cabin. This was not going to be a cake walk however, as the crew went over the details starting two days before the EVA. All critical systems inside the Thales were checked and re-checked. The suites were tried on and tested over an hour period. Telemetry and cameras were made ready to follow every move of the EVA astronauts. The whole task would take about six hours and would require that the astronauts assemble two 100 foot long skids from carbon fiber reinforced aluminum tubing. The skids would be attached by a multitude of struts and shock absorbers attached to the underside of the spacecraft. The landing weight of the craft would be on the order of 180,000 pounds considering the fuel burn from takeoff and the low gravity on Mars. The approach angle would be about three degrees, about the same as a regular aircraft on earth, however the speed would be significantly higher at 250 knots. This was necessary because the wings of the 747 with full flap deployment would still stall at 240 knots in the Martian atmosphere. So the approach would be fast and touch down hard unless the most delicate of flying was performed. The flight crew had spent many hundreds of hours in the simulators working out the technique and handling emergencies. It would be risky, but one thing in their favor was the choice of landing spots which was selected with great care.

The consensus among planetary astronomers and aerodynamicists was that a long flat area with prominent features would be best. It would be very important for the flight crew to use these visual references during the landing sequence to verify the mission computers' operation. They would have to take over and land if there was any problems, so it was important to make any errors in the approach visually obvious. The most prominent feature on Mars is Olympus Mons, a 15 mile high mountain just above the equator. The flight path was chosen to go over the polar regions to take advantage of the thicker atmosphere for slowing, then aiming straight for the mountain which would be seen from a great distance. As the spacecraft slowed down and the mountain grew closer the spacecraft would execute a left hand turn to align itself to aim between two less prominent mountains, Ascraeus Mons and Pavonis Mons, also near the equator. Between the mountains is a long flat plain of featureless Martian soil named Tharsis

Montes. This flat area is like a huge Bonneville Salt Flat lake bed but 400 miles long. The crew would be able to easily discern the two mountains and plan to touch down exactly even with both. Taking a southeasterly heading the spacecraft would slide on the surface for many miles as it slowed down using lift spoilers and parachute deployment. The sensation of landing would feel the same as landing a jetliner on earth only the speed would be significantly higher and roll out longer. The flight crew trained for contingencies ranging from un marked boulders to changes in surface friction. Piloting skill would still be necessary to insure a safe landing as was the experience of the astronauts as they landed on the Moon in the 60's and 70's.

But first things first, the EVA team needed to suit up and do their work. This in itself would take an hour with all of the attachments and tests needed to insure safe operation. Benjamin and Judi started reviewing the EVA several hours ahead of time and talked again about the choreography of their movements. After reviewing their actions they moved into the EVA prep room which held the space suits, helmets and backpacks. Stephen and Nanci were waiting there for them and had already started testing the radios and other backpack systems. Although these were safe proven suits, the astronauts did not take anything for granted.   All seams were checked and electrical connections were securely fastened. They were of the American style with pants and top (as apposed to the Russian, which is single piece and has a rear entry door). After a careful donning, the astronauts temporarily put their helmets on and did a five minute pressure check. After passing this test they removed their helmets and put the back packs on and connected the hoses and electrical connections. Again they paused for a systems check and paid particular attention to the safety backup oxygen and communications features. These systems tested, they then attached their helmets and visors and performed a final pressure test. Once ready, the EVA crew entered the air lock for a five minute pressurization cycle. After the timer went off and the gauges showed zero air pressure, the outside door was unlocked and opened. For the EVA crew the view was incredible, for they had not gone "outside" in many weeks. It was just wide open space and millions of parsecs worth of it. They both smiled, now able to stretch their legs. First out was Judy who attached an umbilical cord to a safety ring near the outside of the hatch. The cord was thin but very strong and could be used in an emergency if her suit thrusters did not work or other problems arose. There were a series of hand holds that had been attached to side of the fuselage while on earth, Judy pulled herself along on these holds until she was well clear of the hatch.

Benjamin followed her out and paused to look at the vista, "stunning", he thought. He also attached an umbilical and moved on out into space.

Part of their duties while outside would be to examine the entire spacecraft for any signs of damage during the high vibration acceleration into low earth orbit. Both astronauts had a checklist that scrolled on their PDAs that had to be followed during their EVA; as a result of the MDRS crew's experience with attached PDAs the two astronauts had styluses attached to their index fingers to push the buttons. These styluses would come in handy for other uses as well.

Benjamin and Judy made their way to the forward cargo door on the fuselage. As they did this the crew remaining in the spacecraft had depressurized this portion of the cargo hold in anticipation of the door opening.

"Cargo Hold one pressure to zero," announced Stephen through the EVA suit radio.

"Roger that, Cargo Hold one pressure to zero," repeated Benjamin.

If there was any pressure left in the cargo hold, it would keep the big access door from opening. So Benjamin floated himself in front of the door opening mechanism and opened the access panel to the door controls. Inside the recessed control cavity were several switches and indicator lights. Also inside was a valve handle the size of a door knob. His first action was to turn the valve from the closed position to the open position; this would allow any residual pressure to escape. There was a slight hiss (that only the inside crew could hear) and Benjamin waited until the zero pressure indicator light was illuminated. Next he unlocked the door retaining clamps by pressing the door lock release switch. Again the inside crew heard the mechanism move to the open position. After the unlocked indicator light illuminated he could now engage the door actuating motors. He pressed the final switch and the door started to open inward at a slow pace. The whole exercise would take seven minutes but the last few moments would allow the astronauts to enter the cargo hold and start the extraction of the landing skid components.

Judy went in first and floating to her right moved to the first pallet attached to the floor. She unlatched the access door and opening it slowly, finding the necessary parts for assembly. Each tube that made up the skid assembly was about 10 feet long and had attachment interfaces on both ends. All tubes were numbered and placed inside the cargo container in such a way as to come out sequentially. The tubes also had an attachment mooring that had a ring inserted in it. Judy's first job would be to locate and extract a long wire with a multitude of clips attached to it, The clips would hold each tube in sequence and allow all of the parts to come out without being lost. The assembly wire as it was called was found and it's end was attached to a mooring ring near the entrance to the cargo hold. One by one the tubes were extricated and attached to the assembly wire and slowly allowed to go outside. Benjamin made sure that every part was secure and the whole menagerie was manipulated in such a way as to not hit anything outside. The whole process proceeded smoothly and soon 12 tubes were attached like fish on a clip line and out the door. This would allow the building of the port skid. Other tubes were attached to the astronauts that would connect the fuselage to the skids. The whole assembly would fit together and attach tightly. Benjamin and Judy would assemble the port skid first then return for the parts to construct the starboard skid. Finally the assembly wire would be used with one other to comprise a cross skid brace system.

They worked for several hours before the bulk of the assembly was complete.

"How are you doing, getting tired?" asked Benjamin of Judy.

"A little tired but ok to finish. This was very close to our sims in the underwater tank at NASA," said Judy.

"Yeah, I was thinking the same thing. Cap com,

how is our schedule going?" asked Benjamin.

"You are 17 minutes ahead of schedule, why don't you guys take a break and rest a while. Take in the scenery, cause your heart rates are a little high," instructed the commander.

"Roger that, we'll take a break," answered Benjamin.

With that the two astronauts stopped their physical exertions and simply floated for a few minutes. The view was awe inspiring. All of the stars were out of course and if they drifted into the shadow of a wing they could see the milky way without internal reflections from the sun hitting their helmets. They could also sense that it was a lot colder in the shade as their suits responded with heat. The opposite was true in the sunlight, the stars were harder to see and the suits soon started cooling the astronauts.

Just for fun, the two astronauts floated to the leading edge of one of the wings and sat down with their legs drooping over the edge of the leading edge slat. They sat there thinking about how there were moving at 47,000 miles an hour (and decelerating) while they felt no wind. The earth was a bright blue orb that had diminished in size greatly since their start several weeks ago. Behind them the Red Planet was growing larger and somehow seemed to invite them to come and visit.

After a few more minutes of rest the two astronauts moved back to the underside of the great ship and finished their jobs. They performed a careful inspection of the skid assembly and rigging. In addition, they worked their way around the whole spacecraft looking for any damage. The whole process took another 30 minutes but before long, they found themselves back at the cargo hold. Judy went inside to secure any loose items and close the container that held the skid parts. After she was done, she came out and Benjamin closed the large cargo door, locked it and reset the valve to allow the cargo hold to pressurize again. Before they left that area, Benjamin called the commander and told him of the door's status. Stephen started the pressurization process and announced that the seal on the door was good and they could now come in.

The astronauts floated back to the air lock, entered and sealed the door behind them. After another five minutes of pressurizing, they could open the inside door and re-enter the spacecraft cabin. The suits were turned off and they slowly removed the bits and pieces. Once out they both looked like they had run a marathon. Stephen and Nanci had arrived to help and store the equipment.

"How was it Ben?" asked Nanci as she inadvertently kissed Benjamin on the cheek. This had been the first outward show of affection between the two since the "little talk."

After a short awkward moment, Benjamin simply said, "Tiring but fun."

"Actually," continued Judy, not one to ignore the obvious, "It was great, it was nice to get out for a stroll."

They finished putting the equipment away and went back into the common area where candy bars and coffee were awaiting the EVA team. There was a complete de-briefing, going over the details of the assembly and spacecraft inspection. After that, the inside crew made dinner and everyone relaxed a bit. Now they were ready to land, and their thoughts moved to getting ready for the re-entry, which would be coming up soon.

Chapter 10: Time to get back to gravity

"I have Olympus Mons in sight and on radar, it's huge!"

After a few more days the mission flight plan called for the preparation for landing. This meant a complete internal inspection and the stowing of every loose item. Considering the internal size of the spacecraft, this was no easy chore. The crew broke up into teams and started from each end of the fuselage. They would work their ways to the center, cross and then inspect from that point to the other end. There probably were 500 pieces of equipment to store. These included everything in the laboratory, cockpit, crew quarters, storage bins, common area and cargo holds. The work took a full two days, where upon the crew felt like they were getting behind and needed to rush to finish. After a little hustling, they finished the clean up and inspection. The flight plan now called for the re-distribution of fuels and other liquids. This caused the spacecraft to change it's center of gravity and the RCS system responded accordingly to keep the flight path accurate.

The radar systems on board were starting to paint surface details of Mars at this point. The mission computer located Olympus Mons for navigation verification. The infrared and visual sensors were also aligning themselves. Thales was starting to wake up and prepare for the approach. The speeds were now settling down to planned numbers. Attitude was good. Because they had been going faster than expected the ion rockets had to be on a little longer. 24 hours before touchdown, the ion engines shut down and the big ship turned about to face Mars which was just about to fill the forward facing windows.

They were to enter the atmosphere near the South

pole and streaking across the Southern and Northern hemispheres, would go over the North pole. At this point the atmospheric drag should have slowed down the spacecraft enough to allow it to descend below 50,000 feet and head for Olympus Mons, again near the Equator. The final descent would be toward the base of the great mountain, then a 45 degree left hand turn to final approach. The mission computer was now starting to show the lead rectangles that indicated the spacecraft was on course and at the planned speed. Phobos and Deimos where clearly visible rotating slowly about the planet.

12 hours to go, activity increased; all safety systems were checked and a last run through of the cabin was performed. Breakfast was served in zero g for the last time on this leg of the flight. Mars was definitely getting larger in the windows and all of the crew members were starting to get a little anxious. Stephen went so far as to look in all of the electronic equipment cabinets for loose wires or other out of place objects. He also looked under the flight deck and avionics bays. Benjamin secured the laboratory, cargo bays and reviewed the flight plan. Judy took care of the common area and staterooms. Finally, Nanci secured the centrifuge and aft cabin area.

Six hours to go, lunch was served to a slightly distracted crew. They instead chose to review the flight plan and choreograph the landing sequence. Everyone now was excited and happy, geographic features again, dirt rocks, dust; it is amazing what someone can miss when not in contact with home. As usual, e-mails were sent although somewhat shorter than before as the crew wanted to get ready for re-entry. All the earth bound families and friends wished good luck. Mission Control started to increase in activity and more people showed up on the video monitors that sent pictures back to the Thales.

Two hours to go, snack, clean up and taking their stations, the crew had time to contact mission control for an update.

"Thales, mission control, we have good telemetry on you and have you tracking less than .1 degrees off in all axis. All systems are go from here and we wish you good luck."

And after several minutes:

"Mission Control, this is Thales we roger your last transmission, approach descent checklist is complete, we are now getting suited up, all systems nominal."

Several more minutes.

"Thales mission control, we copy your systems as nominal and telemetry concurs. We have a message from the White House and the American people: Good luck and God speed."

Mars Life

"Mission control, Thales, thank you from the crew of the Thales, we appreciate all that you have done for us."

One hour from landing. The crew had their suits on now and had checked them. All members were at their stations and going through the approach check lists. Judy and Nanci accessed the nose camera monitors to watch the show, the two crew members on the flight deck with the best view did not have time to look out the windows as they were going through the final approach checklists.

30 minutes from landing. The spacecraft flew over the South pole of Mars, a very slight buffeting could be felt. The Doppler radar systems recorded a very slight decrease in speed as well. They were on the glide path, all systems were functioning perfectly. In the southern hemisphere they descended further until the buffeting increased a bit more. The rate of speed decreased more and more. The skin temperature of the spacecraft started to increase. The mission computer would judge the rate of descent based on the skin temperature and speed of the spacecraft. So far, everything was by the numbers as they crossed the equator and headed into the Northern hemisphere. The buffeting remained the same as they descended at 20,000 feet per minute. Their speed was the passing through 600 miles per hour now and the airspeed indicator and pressure altimeter came to life. These would be emergency use only

instruments as the radar systems were far more accurate.

15 minutes from landing. Now they were approaching the North pole where the air would be cooler and denser. This fact allowed them to descent yet further into the atmosphere. They were now the equivalent of 200,000 feet and 500 miles per hour. Skin temperature was allowed to increase to it's maximum safe limits and the buffeting increased enough to be noticeable. Looking outside, Judy saw the wing tips move up and down with the bumps, which were not uncomfortable. They rounded the pole passing through 150,000 feet and slowing to 300 miles per hour. The aerodynamic pressure on the ship was now allowing it to fly and the control surfaces started to come alive with movement. According to the airspeed indicator the ship was going 100 miles per hour and increasing. As the ship descended, this speed would increase to the point of allowing the flaps, slats, spoilers, and speed brakes to be used. This was due to the increasing density of the atmosphere, which by the way was warming up now. They would regulate the indicated (not the true) airspeed at 160 miles per hour once the altitude allowed. At that time they would start increasing the surface area of the wing using flaps and slats.

"We are coming up on S1 speed, slowing to capture, we are now captured and stable, Flaps one please," announced the commander.

"Flaps one, aye.   Temperature nominal, speed steady, navigation good, we should see the mountain soon," replied the pilot.

"Flaps two now and arm speed brakes."

"Flaps two aye, speed brakes armed, hydraulic pressure good."

"Lets go for flaps three, I am going to do a gentle bank now."

"Flaps three aye, control surfaces responding, I have the mountain now."

"Good descent rate, I have the mountain too, flaps four please."

"Flaps four aye, glide path good, speed good, slats extended."

"She's flying kinda mushy, just like sim, back on autopilot."

"Ok, glide path still good, speed good, coming through 30,000 feet."

"That's one large mountain, man, coming up on bank maneuver."

"Roger, we are starting to bank, speed good, glide slope good, turn rate one degree per second."

"Coming around to A and P." This was the Commander's shorthand for Ascraeus and Pavonis Mons.

"Coming out of the bank, glide slope good, speed good."

"Landing zone identified, let's try to land on the third stripe". (aircraft instructor's joke)

"Third stripe aye, (smiling) speed good, 5,000 feet altitude 20 miles to threshold."

"GPR (Ground Penetrating Radar) is reading good soil density."

"Looks like there are a few bumps out there, MCC is correcting flight path, 3,000 feet, 10 miles."

"10 miles, final approach check."

"Final approach check, all systems nominal, your on the ball, crew set, 2,000 feet, good speed, five miles."

"Five miles, density still looks good, glide slope three degrees."

"1,000 feet, two miles."

"Two miles."

"500 feet, one mile, good gauges."

"One mile."

"200 feet, 100, 50, 20, touchdown."

"Touchdown, parachutes out, RCS on reverse, spoilers deployed."

"240 knots and coming down."

"Density looks good, skids are good."

"200 knots and slowing."

"Density still good, RCS good."

"150 knots.....100.......50.........20........all stop."

"All stop, lets secure."

"Roger, after landing checklist out."

With that, the large spacecraft had slowed to a stop, amidst a great swirl of red Martian dust. Because of the wing tip vortices and thin air, the dust behind the ship curled up and over the spacecraft in slow motion. From afar it looked like a scorpion's tail rearing up to attack. As the tip of the tail floated over the front of the ship, it also descended, sparkling in the sunlight. The crystalline sparkles were more dense than snowflakes and moved a bit slower as well. Stephen sat in the new found gravity and looked out the cockpit window. The scene reminded him of a wonderful passage in James Joyces's great book 'Dubliners':

"It had begun to snow again. He watched sleepily the flakes, silver and dark, falling obliquely against the lamplight. The time had come for him to set out on his journey westward. Yes, the newspapers were right: snow was general all over Ireland. It was falling on every part of the dark central plain, on the treeless hills, falling softly upon the Bog of Allen and, further westward, softly falling into the dark mutinous Shannon waves. It was falling, too, upon

every part of the lonely churchyard on the hill where Michael Furey lay buried. It lay thickly drifted on the crooked crosses and headstones, on the spears of the little gate, on the barren thorns. His soul swooned slowly as he heard the snow falling faintly through the universe and faintly falling, like the descent of their last end, upon all the living and the dead."

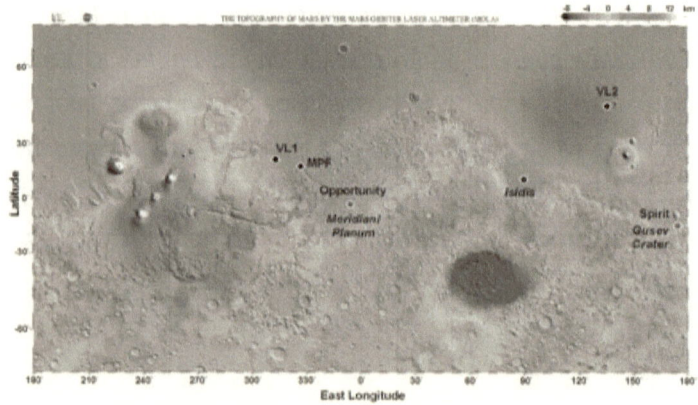

Chapter 11: A new home

"Touchdown! This is exactly where they landed."

The crew sat silent, looking out the windows, Thales hummed and murmured, getting bored from inactivity. The great craft had worked flawlessly, calculating all parameters billions of times over. Computers still chatted amongst themselves at a billion words per second. It was time to give her a rest, and the flight crew started to shut non-essential systems down one by one.

"Star scanner off."

"Ion engine main system off."

"Navigation radar system off."

"GPR off."

161

Mars Life

"Navigation computers off."

"Beacon on."

"Telemetry good."

"Mission Control, this is Thales, we have landed safely and come for all mankind in peace, it is on the shoulders of the great efforts and encouragement of the people on earth. We come here proudly to represent all of you, and invite you to follow."

After a multi-minute delay:

"Thales, this is mission control, we copy you down, telemetry is good. All the people of earth extend their congratulations."

Pleasantries aside, this did not feel like the landing on the moon. It was not that inhospitable a place without any atmosphere or hope. It felt like home in a way. It just needed a bit of work to make it more comfortable. Sort of like moving into a run down house without heat and a few broken windows. One thing at a time now and it would all work out. The environment of comfort would start with a few people working on primitive shelters, joined later by more settlers with more work energy to make yet a better place to live. Finally, a hoard of people representing all levels of society and skills. The first get the dirtiest and the last complain the most..... such is life.

"Ok, lets secure all systems, follow your checklist

completely, we will soon be outside for a walk," remarked the commander.

The crew felt a bit better with some gravity now, which also made it feel like home. They could walk down the corridor in the cabins and cockpit. It genuinely was a relief to have the sense of up and down. The crew smiled amongst themselves again.

All system secured, communication established and everything safe, the crew could now seriously consider going outside. They would be the first people to do so, only robots had preceded them. There was a significant nuance though, regarding how it would happen. It really did not matter who went first, although all four of them thought it would be cool to do so. The best thing would be for all of them to do it at the same time, symbolic as it were. Stephen recognized this fact long before they even left earth and had planned for it. There was no reason not to do it any other way, and certainly no one would complain about the decision.

"Ok, here's the deal, everyone suit up, check out each other's safety systems and we will lower the air-stairs. We will all go down to the surface together and at the exact same time. How does that sound?" asked Stephen.

"Perfect," thought and enunciated the other crew members. No one is special here, considering the feelings

163

the crew had for each other and more importantly, the symbolic nature of representing everyone on earth. There really was no other way.

Preparations were made, suits were donned, the air-stair was extended and they all moved out to the platform even with the hatch. They stopped momentarily to take in the view, eager to touch the soil, they soon found their way down to the lower platform. Looking left and right to each of their crew member, they joined hands and jumped the remaining 12 inches. A cloud of dust slowly rose to meet them but by the time it would have impeded their vision they were off in different directions exploring the new land.

The land was soft and red and to some degree reminded Stephen about the MDRS experience in Utah. He thought now about the MDRS crew and how they were feeling as the world now knew that humans were on Mars. They had done so much to allow this mission to succeed. He would bring something special back for all of them. But for now he had to keep track of the wandering crew members who were having a great time looking around in the low gravity. The geologic specimens were to be collected first followed by the deployment of several experimental packages. This work needed to be done quickly, just in case they needed to get back into the spacecraft due to a safety issue or other unexpected danger.

"Let's keep to our schedules everybody," announced Stephen through the GMRS transceiver.

Judy and Nanci went over to the cargo door and went through the procedure to open it. A platform was pulled out and they ascended to locate the experiment packages. Benjamin immediately started taking sample bags out of his suit pockets and filling them with dirt or diggings from the side of a large rock or ledge. He numbered them and included a waypoint on the pseudo GPS system that he had strapped to his arm. The initial survey would be to retrieve as many diverse samples as possible from the surrounding area. Later he and the rest of the crew would make careful geological surveys.

All crew members had cameras and were recording both audio and visual information. The radio channel was open from each crew member to the spacecraft as well, letting the people back home listen in on the rapid list of discoveries being made.

They had landed at noon, Martian time and considering the time of year, had about six more hours of work to do before sunset. The Martian day is 24 hours 39.5 minutes long and they had decided to implement the ideas of Kim Stanley Robinson in <u>Red Mars</u> and just allow the clocks to stop at midnight for 39.5 minutes. They would call this "free time" and joke that they would not age during that period. Any transgressions could not be recorded either and of course Benjamin and Nanci would try to take advantage of this fact. Nothing harmful of course, just playful.

The crew did their immediate chores, storing the sample bags in the cargo hold and deploying and activating the science experiments. They then took a break, sitting on small boulders and sipping water.

"This is absolutely great," said Benjamin. "It is better than I expected, and I expected a lot!"

"I can hardly wait to assemble the hab and greenhouse," followed Judy.

What she meant by this was that when these structures were complete and tested, the crew could go inside and open their visors (using cannulas) , while looking through the transparent plastic sheeting that made up the various rooms. They would easily be able to see out. The wind, even when over 50 miles per hour would only be felt as a gentle breeze. They had brought 10 rooms worth of plastic sheeting. The rooms had been pre-assembled to be placed on the surface, pressurized with warm air, connected together and occupied. There was over 10,000 square feet of living and greenhouse space. Martian dirt would be brought inside and compacted to make up the base of the floors. Later, the dirt would be mixed with an efficient cement compound that would be smoothed for the flooring in the living spaces. Eventually, they would try to make bricks out of the soil itself, however this would require finding water.

Water was therefore everything. The principle activities for the next few months would center around finding water. The satellites that had preceded them sensed it's existence. The rovers had found evidence as well, and the geologists back on earth were convinced that the walls of craters and parts of the ice caps must have had water at one time. The best guess was that there was water just under the surface in crystalline form and/or many kilometers down in pockets. They had the equipment to find out where it was located and hopefully harvest it. Obviously the discovery of water on Mars would ignite a flurry of future missions, and of course permanent habitation. Armed with this task, the best possible equipment to find it, and personal interests, the crew worked hard starting in these very first hours of habitation to find any evidence of water. They took several 10 foot deep core samples for later study, and rolled over several rocks for additional samples. Then they dug into some crater walls to take more samples.

Over the next few weeks the "buildings" needed to

be assembled and moored down. Then the rovers and balloons would be used to examine the area of 100 square miles around them to take pictures and sniff the air for hydrogen molecules (one of the signatures of water). Finally, EVA trips would be taken to take core samples and dig under the surface to look for the precious fluid.

But today was special, too full of excitement to start serious work. After a few hours, Stephen and Nanci went back inside the Thales to rest and start recording sample information.

"What a wonderful place geologically," started Nanci.

"It wasn't as cold as I thought it would be, felt actually warm in places," continued Stephen.

Due to the thin atmosphere, dark pieces of equipment could absorb solar radiation and warm up many degrees. Inside the greenhouse they would experiment with black colored plates that would heat up and thereby warm the air in the greenhouse. While inside the spacecraft, Nanci took several sample bags sealed in air tight containers and attached the valved vent line attachments to a gas chromatograph to examine the warming dirt for chemical emissions. This was done obviously for safety reasons but also for the first signs of water. After the samples were deemed safe they were examined under a standard microscope and finally under a scanning electron microscope to catalog the fine rock and crystalline structures found in the soil. The pictures and gas chromatograph findings were sent immediately back to earth for further analysis and comment. Stephen checked out the spacecraft systems and prepared for the rest of the crew's return.

As Nanci was examining the samples Stephen asked, "Hey Nanci, find anything interesting?"

"It's all very interesting, rock structures indicate the presence of volcanic activity, erosion and the crystals are like gypsum in some ways. The gas chromatograph indicates the presence of the chemicals we were expecting and a small amount of trace hydrogen. I sent the results back to the geologists on earth for comment, we should hear in the next few hours," she answered.

Meanwhile, Stephen had finished taking core samples and Judy was finishing up activating the science packages and pointing the high gain antennas. She also starting thinking about a good place to start building the first structure. But by this time they were both getting a bit tired and decided to go back into the spacecraft to rest and examine their samples. They moved toward the spacecraft and after climbing the stairs, entered the airlock one by one to pressurize up to ship pressure. After the five minute cycle

169

they entered the EVA room and began to vacuum each other off, as did Stephen and Nanci an hour before. Completing that chore, they took off their suits and proceeded inside to meet the others.

"Is this a great place or what," asked Benjamin.

"It is amazing, the geology is just amazing," replied Judy.

"We're going to discover more about Mars in the next 24 hours than anyone has in history," said Benjamin.

"I know," replied Judy, "It's nice that the people on earth will discover these things along with us."

They found their way back to the others and started to talk excitedly about their findings. After about an hour, the sun began to set in the West. As it moved toward the horizon they noticed that it was a bit smaller that on earth, less than ½ degree wide. It was almost as bright though, due to the thin atmosphere. At about five minutes before it disappeared, they noticed thin tendrils of Martian dust that had formed into very long dust devils that reached high into the sky. They moved very slowly in ballet like style across the horizon. As the sun descended below the horizon, these tendrils also disappeared. The stars came quickly and were very bright and colorful due to the thin atmosphere. The stars were so bright in fact that locating a constellation was a chore. The Milky Way was very easy to discern as were several of the planets that happened to be up. Jupiter in particular, being several million miles closer at this point in the orbit, was particularly bright and upon later outside examination actually cast a shadow. The crew slowly drifted away from the windows to continue work and ate at their work stations. The core samples were safety tested and then a few slices were examined with the lab equipment. The first thing the scientists noticed was that the soil was stratified into several distinct layers. These were probably built up from several significant dust storms over the past several hundred years. Again the gas chromatograph results showed the basic soil constituents as well as trace gaseous elements including hydrogen.

"It's too early to tell what we have," said Judy, "And we are still waiting for a comment from the geologists on earth. The deeper the core sample, the more the trace elements indicate the presence of hydrogen, but it still very dry."

"We have a lot of work to do," said Stephen.

The crew worked late into the night and after returning to their staterooms, slept very well. This was due in part from the excitement and hard work during the day but also to the fact that there was now some gravity and it felt a lot like earth.

They arose the next morning to a brilliant sunrise,

ate breakfast and planned their activities. A weather station was brought out and turned on, there would be many of these deployed every 15 miles or so on future EVAs, they would talk amongst each other and relay the weather information from all of the stations back to the Thales for plotting and telemetry back to earth. They would be able to see frontal passage and soon predict the conditions that would lead to a dust storm.

They also pulled out several solar panels for hab power. These were set up and activated in anticipation of the inflating of the hab. A fuel processor of Zubrin's design was also pulled out and activated. It immediately started to make the fuel necessary for the trip back home and was attached through pressure hoses to the fuel tanks aboard the Thales. Finally, a CO_2 'cracker' was brought out and deployed. It broke apart the CO_2 molecule to get oxygen for the hab and with the trace hydrogen found so far in the soil and air would combine to make water. The hydrogen and oxygen was also stored to send to the fuel cells in the Thales to make electricity and ship's water.

The first hab assembly was brought out and laid on the surface. The perimeter was staked down temporarily and the output of the 'cracker' was attached to slowly inflate it, which would take a few days.

The crew, when inside continued to examine

172

samples and cores for geological purposes as well as the search for water. The geologists from earth finally sent a message saying that the findings so far indicated that trace water in the form of ice was in evidence. They felt that there should be crystal deposits somewhere in larger amounts and made several suggestions as to where to look. They noted that the soil constituents indicated a long and complex geological history that included volcanic activity, much erosion and significant fluid flows of water and later, carbon dioxide. The amount of solar radiation and cosmic ray bombardment over the millennia had caused compound breakdowns and any living organism on the surface would have a very hard time surviving. Second to finding water on the Mars, the crew also looked for evidence of life, which was predicted to be microbial in nature and well protected from the elements. This meant that any of the potential organisms would be found far under the surface, buried under rocks or in the crater walls. During the searches for water the crew and geologists on earth both looked for the telltale signs of life. This was done by looking at cellular byproducts in the form of methane or other carbon based emissions. They also looked for fossil evidence in the form of trails or calcium carbonate deposits. After a few days, the samples and cores started yielding candidates for life and every once in a while a water crystal. They would have to expand their search but now had a trail to follow.

The ATV rovers were brought out and in groups of two, the crew started to explore the area farther away from the spacecraft. The search pattern was initially designed likes spokes of a wheel where the spokes were in 20 degree increments. After several EVAs the sample and core evidence started to show a pattern. They continued until they had filled in the "wheel" to a distance of three miles. The pattern filled in to indicate a subterranean stream bed that had once flowed right past their landing spot. Finding the most promising spots, the crew used the deepest core drilling tools they had. After several hours of hard work the drilling finally finished. The tube was extracted and the sections were taken apart for transport to the spaceship. Inside they were checked for noxious emissions using the gas chromatograph and slices of each section were examined under the microscopes. The depth of the core had exceeded 200 feet and as they examined the slices from deeper and deeper depths they noticed that the amount of water in the form of ice crystals started to increase. At the depth of 200 feet the core samples indicated that had not yet found the peak of the water abundance but even so had enough to be able to heat up and slowly extract. Stephen and Judy worked on a plan to place an electric tape heater on the end of the core sample

174

tube, run it back down the sample hole and try to pump up the liquid after a period of heating. The heater tape and pump mechanism was activated during the day by solar panel. During the next few days the crew placed the core sampler tube back in the hole and varied the time to pump cycle until they had an optimum flow, which was about a cup per hour. The water was pumped into a plastic holding tank that was placed in the first plastic room, now inflated. After careful analysis the water was deemed safe and after a gallon was extracted, the crew each had a cup during dinner.

"Not bad," pronounced Nanci, "It tastes like stream water."

They let the water pump system work for several days and started to accumulate a fair amount of emergency water. But the crew knew that soon the pumping process would need to be expanded, either by digging deeper or finding water crystals in other, easier to get places. They could also try to super heat the area below. Thinking creatively, they decided to use the residual heat from the propellant production plant and the excess electric current available from the ship. By conserving lights and heat during the evening, the amount of residual electric energy was considerable. After a week of tweaking, the water pump was putting out almost a gallon an hour. Now the problem was going to be how to store the excess water.

"It's time to try and make bricks," announced Stephen. "Let's see if we can use some of the water with the soil and see how it holds up. The water will freeze outside and we might be able to make ice cube bricks."

After several tries a recipe of Martian soil and a bit of water was found. The bricks could be melted later to re-extract the water but for now they could start making walls. The process became efficient with Martian mud being placed in forms made of plastic and left outside. Using this technique, the crew made 30 to 40 bricks a cubic foot in size per day. The bricks were light weight due to the Martian gravity and assembly was very easy. The first several structures were 10 foot high domes to cover the propellant plant and water pump station. Once the bricks were in place they used a small water bottle to squirt fluid into the cracks and act like mortar. The assembly went quickly and soon they found themselves trying to think of new structures to build. They discovered also that if they placed a plastic sheet over the domes, any minor water evaporation would be minimized. Also, they found that the heat generated by the various equipment inside the domes slowly heated the insides up and in the case of the propellant production plant, the temperature rose above 50 degree Fahrenheit. Now it was beginning to be fun. Would a double walled structure be insulated enough to live in? What would happen if a large dome was eventually made over the water pump station, would it heat up enough to draw the water to the surface and make a pond?

"Let's build a city," proclaimed Benjamin during dinner one evening. The other crew members smiled knowing that it could be done.

"No, I mean let's really build a city," Benjamin said in a more serious tone.

"You know we can't do that Ben," replied Stephen, "We have a pretty tight schedule to follow, and preparations for the return trip to consider."

"I think there is life here," interjected Nanci, "I think we need to spend some serious time looking for more and cultivating the microbes I have just found."

"When did this conversation get out of control?" asked Stephen, a little annoyed. "We all have duties to perform and it is going to be a squeeze now considering all of the detours we have taken. Mission control is noticing our delays and asking me to explain them. It's all well and good that we can make structures and conserve heat and pump water, but we are not here on a vacation, we have a lot of serious work to do, and I expect everyone to do their part. Silence followed this statement and Benjamin and Nanci looked at each other briefly in a way that conveyed an alternate direction of thought.

The next morning, Benjamin awoke at five in the morning. Unable to return to sleep, he stared out the window and thought about how much they had discovered about this place. He thought about how this place was not as intimidating as everyone had thought; it was more like finding yourself in the middle of Siberia, cold, inhospitable but not impossible for habitation. Using your wits, you could make a safe warm place to live, there certainly is water, and maybe a way to grow and cultivate food. His mind wandered about the possibilities until the sun rose in the East. His last thoughts about the subject were about how lonely it would be after a while, and maybe a very long while if he never received any visitors.

The crew gathered for breakfast and made plans for the day. At this point they were coming up on the midpoint of their stay and like reaching mid flight, had to now turn their attention to finishing up their surveys and other experiments. Stephen and Benjamin had to start thinking about preparing Thales for the return flight. They still had a few months to go, but slowly they had to prepare to leave. It had been a great adventure for the whole crew, and the members felt like they did not want to cross that line of ceasing the adventure in favor of reminiscing. Although there was still time to enjoy the surroundings, the crew members would pause every once in a while to try to burn an image or sensation in their brains for later retrieval.

A few days later, on an EVA to the South, the Benjamin and Nanci found a rather large cave situated in a horseshoe shaped formation of Martian "sandstone." The opening faced to the South and the whole area (several acres worth) received sunlight for most of the day. The formation was actually the side of a mountain that had been carved away by millennia of erosion. The cave was situated in the back center of the formation and was several thousand square feet in size with a 10 foot opening in the center, tendrils running back to more opened "rooms" inside. Ben and Nanci explored the cave in a scientific fashion for about an hour, and at one point stood at the entrance looking to the south. The sun was high in the sky and it's warmth was heating the insides of the pair's helmets.

"This is nice," reflected Nanci.

"Yeah, we could put the swimming pool over there," joked Benjamin pointing to his left.

"And the garden over there," continued Nanci.

They both paused for a moment reflecting whimsically. But then a serious thought was borne at that moment in both of them. It could happen, they could build a greenhouse, they could seal off the entrance of the cave with a "windowed" airlock. They could pressurize the inside of the cave and live in it and build a domed house outside; they could have water and heat and communications with earth, grow food, and they could have an observatory and a laboratory and children.... They could stay.

"We need to talk, Nanci," implored Benjamin.

"Do you think we could do it, survive?" asked Nanci.

"I think so," replied Benjamin, "It would be risky at first, no backups. We would have to have all of our share of food on Thales brought to the cave; we would also have to have every last bit of equipment from the ship that is not needed for their return voyage. We would have to make sure we had a large reserve of water, medical supplies, clothing. It would be an enormous risk."

"Just like the pioneers in the 1800's," countered Nanci, "Living off the land without any backup; it wasn't easy for them but for the most part they survived."

"Stephen is going to flip out if we decide to do this, you know," said Benjamin.

"Well, I don't think he and Judy are going to be terribly shocked, in a way they also want to stay here as well but they are being drawn back by family and duty. It's really our decision you understand," countered Nanci.

"Yeah, your right about that," followed Benjamin.

They remained for a few more minutes and contemplated their decision to stay. It would not be easy indeed. They would have to live on the food they were going to use on the way back, while at the same time grow and cultivate the food necessary to stay for an extended period. There were a lot of unknowns, but they had brought a very large amount of seeds and seedlings. This along with the microbes they might be able to cultivate could give them a year's worth of food. Hopefully, if there was any problem, an unmanned supply ship or even Thales herself could return to replenish their supplies. They would have to shore up the cave first and quickly. Then they would have to get the greenhouses going with water and heat pumped in. After that they could use the Martian bricks to build more permanent shelters.

After the pause, Benjamin and Nanci held gloved hands for a moment and went back to the ATVs to return and tell the rest of the crew the bad news. The drive was a little bit slower this time and as they returned, both of them spent a little extra time securing the vehicles and cleaning up in the EVA room. Inside the main cabin, Stephen and Judy were busy checking samples and documenting the results of another geological survey. Benjamin and Nanci entered the laboratory were the others were and sat down. A silence ensued that became awkward enough for Stephen to say, "What's the matter?"

"Nanci and I want to stay," started Benjamin.

Mars Life

"Well you can't do that, I need you two to help get us home," said Stephen.

"You can make it without us, you know that, we practiced the loss of crew members and how to compensate for it."

"So you two 'pioneers' want to live on the surface of Mars, where no one is going to be able to help you if you get in trouble? Stay here in minimal shelter with a finite amount of food, staking your lives of whether or not you can grow more? You want to stay here not knowing if the water we found is going to run out? And, luckily Judy and I get to go home to face a firing squad for not following orders? Our careers would be over, I will never fly again and probably have to change our names to protect our families. Nice idea, is this all yours Stephen? Did you talk Nanci in to this nonsense?" By this time Stephen was red faced. Judy listened quietly, she was not happy about the selfish behavior as well, but wanted to hear the other side before she would comment. Stephen was up and pacing about trying to control his anger but in reality this revelation did not come as a shock to either Stephen or Judy.

"We just feel very strongly about this," started Benjamin. "We have no intention of getting you two in trouble, but Nanci and I want to try this, we think we can make it. You are right about us being selfish but so were the

182

pioneers, they made the same choices that we are, we feel it in our blood. It seems like a natural thing for us to do, I didn't try to convince Nanci about staying. It just happened, it makes sense to her as well, to try. We have to do this Stephen, if we don't we will never be given the chance to do it again. As far as the logistics..............

"As far as the logistics Benjamin...," interrupted Stephen. "You will need all of the extra food on board the Thales including the emergency rations. Don't look shocked Ben, Judy and I have been talking about this and frankly I am amazed you said something so early. I expected you to tell us an hour before liftoff. I and probably Judy, don't like your decision but your are in charge of your own destiny. We didn't think that we would be able to talk you out of it so we have to plan 'your escape' carefully. I think that it is very risky to try to do this, mission control is going to be very upset, especially with us. But considering that there is a chance you could make it, they might consider another mission to either rescue you or join you, I don't know which. You two have to be completely sure you want to do this, and understand that you might die for your experiment."

"We understand," said Nanci, obviously relieved, "we know the dangers and are willing to try and make it."

"Thanks Stephen," said Benjamin, "we both appreciate your open minds about this."

Mars Life

"You know," said Judy, "this really all hinges on whether or not you can make things grow here. I suggest that we spend a lot of extra time trying to understand what will grow and you two 'pioneers' had better understand that if we cannot make any progress on the greenhouses and food, that you are coming back with us. If that happens we will make no mention about your wishes to stay."

"Seems reasonable to me," agreed Stephen, "if would be irresponsible of me to knowingly let you get into trouble. Judy and I will do everything in our power to set you up here, but if it looks too dangerous, you two are definitely coming back with us, do you understand?"

"Agreed," said Benjamin with Nanci nodding in the background.

Chapter 12: Making preparations for the big move

"Shut down all system…..look at that!"

For the next several weeks, the crew worked furiously to set up Benjamin and Nanci with a safe place to live. The two scientists spent most of their time in the newly built greenhouses, trying every variation of position, light level and water amount to get the seedlings to grow. It was difficult but eventually they started lettuce, radishes and beans and got them stabilized. In one greenhouse they placed the propellant refinery inside to heat it. It worked well enough the keep the insides above 50 degrees F. They also found that if they placed a wall of bricks inside one the greenhouses, it would warm up during the day and retain it's heat throughout most of the evening without losing too much of its water content. Eventually, methods were found to cultivate the small microbes they had found within the sub-terrainian water. They were not sure that they could eat the mass of greenery that was now growing in the petri dishes, but at the very least it seemed to be producing a large amount of oxygen.

At the end of the furious activity, they had successfully started 15 different plants, including potatoes, tomatoes, wheat, legumes, onions, radishes, beans, and squash. There were a lot of other types of seeds as well, and they would have to try and grow all of them eventually. The water supply seemed steady and was certainly enough to make a large amount of emergency rations.

They pulled everything out of the spaceship that they could leave including the final mystery satellite that was to be deployed in Martian orbit upon their leaving orbit. Oxygen tanks and pumps were unbolted from inside the cabin to leave in case of emergencies. One of the fuel cells was also extricated. One good thing about stripping the ship was that it made it very light for takeoff and would help in the acceleration out of Martian gravity. In all, at least a year's supply of oxygen, water and food could be depended on. The Martian crew would have to make or continually repair all of the essential equipment to survive any longer. It was decided that this was a minimally safe situation, in case of emergency, mission control could probably mount a rescue mission. Stephen and Judy were feeling a bit better about leaving behind the other two. Although they would be getting in trouble, they thought that it would be worth it in the long run, assuming that the Martian crew was successful. They knew that upon return, there would be serious questions to answer, but again it wasn't really their choice. Hopefully they would not end up regretting their decision because of the earth bound peoples' reactions. It certainly would be interesting.

Within three weeks of liftoff the focus changed from making a safe home for Benjamin and Nanci to preparing Thales for the trip home. All items were stored, including a wealth of Martian geology and water. Because they had stripped the ship on non-essential items and were lighter, they had some extra room for more samples. The inside of the main cabin was now rather Spartan considering they had dismantled the walls of the un-needed staterooms and taken out extra chairs. Judy would now ride up in the cockpit with Stephen. They also donated extra space suits and clothing for the Martian pair.

As the launch day grew near, the family grew very close and anticipated that they would all feel very sad upon leaving. They had a few parties during the last days before liftoff, one including a bit of wine that was somehow snuck aboard before leaving earth.

"We are really going to miss you," said Judy, "this has been an amazing and historic voyage. Maybe in the future, you two will be considered heroes."

"We are going to miss you as well, Judy," said Nanci. "It will be very strange at first to be here alone, however for some reason, I am looking forward to it. For a while at least we won't have to pay taxes."

"You have enough communications equipment to keep in constant contact, especially if you take apart the satellite and use it's transmitters," said Stephen. "We will have to test everything before we leave, but do so in a way that does not alert mission control to your plans. After we leave we expect you two to contact us often using the Internet, you are probably going to be the only friends we have left after we return."

They all smiled at this, had a nice meal and went to

sleep.   The next day would be the last together, final preparations and pre-flight operations were done. The fuel refinery had done it's job admirably and the tanks were full. In addition the oxygen in the Thales was also topped off. All systems were thoroughly checked and re-checked and the minimal flight crew felt completely confidant about their return flight. On the ground the "Robinson Crusoes" also got prepared for their stay.   The cave was sealed off temporarily and pressurized. Heaters were place inside and kept the temperature more than comfortable.   During this last day, Benjamin went inside the cave and opened his visor to work for several hours on lighting and safety items. It seemed normal to do so.   The way the entrance was situated below the living quarters allowed oxygen to accumulate inside, so even if there was a breach of the air lock, they would have plenty of time to make repairs. Carbon dioxide was pumped into the greenhouse and oxygen from same was pumped into the cave. The ground crew left most of the test instrumentation to test for these gases.   After a while they would fashion an automatic system to adjust the air inside and warn of any problems. Electricity was in abundance from the solar pods outside. Water had accumulated to more that 700 gallons stored in tanks. All of the equipment necessary to search for more was left as well.

Mars Life

The next morning everyone arose to a beautiful sunrise and started final preparations. This included storing everything and strapping any loose items and equipment down. The work went on in unusual silence. Everyone was thinking of the big changes that were about to occur. The home crew were getting comfortable in their new digs; the flight crew was feeling confidant about the health of the spacecraft. Noon came and everyone sat down to a small lunch. The conversation consisted mostly of small talk until Benjamin clear his throat looked at Stephen and said, "Nanci and I want to get married, as captain of the ship would you do this?"

After a few moments, Stephen said, "Sure....but what about the bachelor party?"

Quickly Benjamin responded, "we're having it." Everyone smiled, the idea of marriage made a lot of sense certainly, considering the true depth of their commitment. It would help sooth any hard feelings on earth upon the flight crew's return. It also made sense also because they would make the whole affair a big party. Obviously they would have to be creative about wedding gowns and tuxedos. More importantly, Stephen had to figure out what to say as their flight plan document did not include the proper words for this procedure. In reality, everyone was done with work and would have a great time preparing for a wedding. After several hours, most of the preparations were done, Stephen put on his best flight suit, Judy put on her's as well. The bride and groom were also dressed the same but somehow their proud behavior made them look more dressed up. The crew had cleaned up the common area, centered the table and strung wiring harnesses around the room. Music was found on the Internet and downloaded. This music played softly in the background of a few happy people on a planet far away, just acting normally. The setting was perfect, love, commitment and sacrifice were to be displayed here now and later for all of the people on earth to admire.

At five o'clock, the ceremony started; Judy led Nanci in her finest from the aft stateroom area up front to the awaiting Stephen and Benjamin. They stopped a few feet away, Judy moved off to her left and faced everyone, Nanci and Benjamin stood in front of Stephen to begin the proceedings.

"We are gathered here today to join these two people in holy matrimony. We are here also to join together in creating a new society started by these two wonderful people. This union is based on love, honor, respect and appreciation. There will be hard times ahead and above all you two have to respect each other's opinions and actions. For now you will not have anyone else but each other. Remember that above all things. You will have our support no matter where we are and the support of the good people of earth. Live long and prosper. Now, do you Benjamin Kenwood take as your bride Nanci Vico as your wedded wife, to hold and respect until death?"

"I do," stated Benjamin.

"And do you Nanci Jameson take as your lawfully wedded husband Benjamin Kenwood to hold and respect until death?"

"I do," followed Nanci.

With this the bride and groom exchanged rings quickly fashioned from silver wire that was wound up and tied into two neat rings. They would last a long time and represent the day of marriage well. The couple exchanged kisses next and shook hands and hugged the remain crew members.

After the ceremony, everyone sat down for dinner and yet another bottle of wine mysteriously stowed away. Later that night, it was finally time to go home. So for the first time in months the crew split up with the new Martian colonists departing to confetti made up of pieces of notepaper. They went to the now warm cave, went through the air lock and turned off the lights.

Thales was a lot quieter and a bit lonelier that night, but it was to be expected. Stephen stayed up a little later that usual to go over the weight and balance calculations.

192

Judy for her part, read a little, stared out the window in anticipation of the journey home and went to sleep.

The next morning, the flight crew heard the unusual action of the air lock first thing. The newlyweds came in for breakfast smiling.

"Our cave is wonderful, considering," said Nanci as everyone laughed.

"I've got a lot to do to make it better, but it is ok for now." continued Benjamin.

They new couple felt a little anxious about the departure of Thales but still determined to try and make it work.

"The mission computer is still capable of changing the weight and balance if you two want to come with us," implored Stephen already knowing the answer.

"No, we will be fine," said Nanci. "It was perfectly comfortable last night, the plants are looking good and we have food and water for months. In fact you two are over extending your welcome."

"Ok, your choice," answered Stephen.

The flight crew did the final preparations for takeoff, initiated the flight directors and autopilots. They brought up all of the ship's power and started the pre-launch check list. At a certain point in the checklist, it became time to seal the hatch. The flight crew came in from the cockpit and met the new colonists for a goodbye.

"A wonderful flight and experience," began Benjamin.

"Yes it was, we will miss you so keep in touch often," said Stephen.

"Best of luck, be safe," continued Judy.

"And you as well, have a great journey back we will talk to you soon," finished Nanci.

With that the colonists moved toward the air lock and donned their suits. Stephen and Judy helped as much as they could. Finally when the colonists were suited up they paused to look at each other and shook hands through the thick gloves. The two colonists went into the air lock, sealed it and started the pump down process. The flight crew stayed and observed through the port hole. After the process was complete, everyone waved and the hatch was closed. The sealing mechanism was initiated and the flight crew went to the cabin to start the flight home.

"It's lonely in here now," said Judy.

"Your right, I hope they will be alright," answered Stephen.

The flight crew did a final walk through pausing to look at the final vestiges of the other members' evidence of life on board. The last napkins and cups were put away, cabinets locked and the lights dimmed for the takeoff.

They strapped in and started running down the checklist.

"APU start."

"APU on and power is in the green."

"Cabin pressurization check."

"Cabin pressure good, all valves closed, cargo hatches closed and locked, crew hatch closed and locked."

"Electrical buses on."

"Electrical buses on, voltage and amps good."

"Hydraulic pressure pumps on."

"Hydraulic pressure pumps on and pressure good."

"Flight controls checked."

"Flight controls check and good, RCS system up and checked good."

"Flaps in take off position."

"Flaps at 40, slats deployed, speed brake in."

"Mission control computer engaged."

"Mission control computer engaged and all warnings out."

"Ok, main engine start sequence."

"Main engine pumps on, igniters on, we have a good start."

"Ok, here we go, throttles coming up."

With a final look outside, Stephen slowly pushed the throttle forward to initiate movement. After the initial thrust up to 50% the large spacecraft started to nudge forward. Then gaining a little speed, Stephen brought back the power to allow the ship to move faster without too much vibration. After they exceeded 50 knots of ground speed, he brought the throttle up to 80%. The ship shuddered but accelerated rapidly. Soon they were moving past 250 knots. Stephen applied back pressure to the control column and the nose slowly rose to a pitch angle of about 10 degrees. He held this pitch angle for a moment as the wings started to work. The great craft lumbered a bit on takeoff but soon was accelerating rapidly. Judy nudged the flaps in at Stephen's command and soon they were clean and climbing at 20,000 feet per second. Looking in the aft facing camera, they saw a 10 mile long horizontal dust devil, spinning slowly from the wake turbulence of the great wings. They continued to climb until reaching a very high orbit. The main engine was shut down and the modified ion engines were engaged. They would not have to orbit the planet for long and soon would be on a trajectory back to earth.

"Mission control this is Thales."

"Thales, mission control, we copy you off and in a good orbit."

"Roger that, main engine is shut down all systems are green, we are looking forward to seeing you soon."

"And, Thales, this is mission control, we have good

telemetry on you except we are not getting any bio readings from crew members Nanci and Benjamin."

"Roger mission control, we understand no bio readings on Benjamin and Nanci, that is because they are not with us, they chose to stay and live on Mars."

Part 2 of Mars Life

The land area of the Earth is approximately equal to the total surface of Mars.

The land area of Africa is about the same as the total surface of the Moon.

Chapter 1: The Voyage Home

"Start looking for the habs"

The spacecraft was sent into high orbit as planned. The radios stayed silent for an unusually long period as the flight controllers on earth mulled over the news of the smaller than anticipated crew on return flight. As one would expect, a multitude of meetings took place starting initially with the flight controllers and mission managers. The news propagated upward to administrators which in turn had meetings with more non flight associated people like lawyers and politicians. Finally, as written reports started to appear, the president was notified and briefed.

It was the decision of these (thousand) people to present the story to the public in such a way as to project a positive light on the developments. Of course, reporters and other interested parties drew conclusions of their own and at once the public was aware of a multitude of opinions regarding the facts of the flight.

"They did not follow the rules,"

"How romantic,"

"What are they really doing?", were some of the conclusions voiced by interested parties.

"How does this effect the future of Mars missions," asked the more scientifically inclined.

As all of the worldwide reactions where being voiced on earth, life on Thales was the antithesis of life at home. The craft had been maneuvered into an optimal trajectory for the return flight of some 6 weeks. The ship was mostly silent with the exception of cooling fans, environmental adjustments made to different parts of the ship and various crew activities. Boredom and silence crept into the ship.

Mars Life

Stephen and Judy did the best they could to keep busy with various experiments and house keeping chores. Six weeks is a pretty long time however, stuck in a ship the size of even a 747. There were few places to explore anymore and the silence of the ship exaggerated the effect of being alone. Four people on board as originally planned made a huge difference in activity level. A crew member would have three other people to interact with not just one.

Although they got along personally and professionally, Stephen and Judy found themselves slowly drifting apart to separate areas of the ship to keep within themselves. Similarly, sailors at sea often experience the same feeling as soon after departure they spend time together talking and standing in close quarters along the railing. After a few days the distance between them stretches to several meters and by the end of a voyage these same sailer's manage to stand as far apart from the others as possible. So too in the Thales; breakfast, lunch and dinner together evolved into just breakfast to go over plans for the upcoming "day". After that Stephen and Judy would find a place to work or nap away from the other. Although the ship's clocks where accurate and set to allow a standard diurnal cycle to occur, the minimal amount of activity causes a slippage in time. The crew found themselves staying up longer and sleeping less. There were continual naps being taken and at any time. The lack of true physical activity allowed their bodies to use their energy longer. Weight loss became a factor as well as subtle changes in their morphology. In space, long duration flight has its hazards with regards to how the human body acclimates to its environment. People become longer, muscles deteriorate and blood re-distributes itself upward away from the legs. This causes puffiness in the face during the initial parts of a space mission. Exercise is mandatory to keep muscle tone and proper movement of blood. But this mission was very long and the crew found themselves not wanting to exercise. Tension grew as mission control became more and more adamant about timing slips and crew activities.

"Thales this is mission control, how do you copy?"

After a long silence......

"This is Thales, go ahead."

"Uh, Thales, the flight physicians are reporting to us that you have missed several exercise sessions, can you confirm?"

"Roger Houston, we have been.....busy working on changes to the equipment. Go ahead."

"OK, Thales we copy you are working on the exercise equipment, please advise us of your changes as soon as possible, we need you to get back to a regular schedule. All of you regular telemetry appears nominal, Over."

"Roger that Houston. We copy. Will advise on changes. We could use some more music and video up links if you can arrange for that."

"Roger Thales, we will make the Internet available on your data channel B. You will notice a few changes regarding the news of your mission."

"OK Houston we will check it out, Thales out."

The diurnal cycles kept slipping until they were 12 hours off of "normal" time. This could not be helped considering the lack of activities. Houston attempted to help with new activities but the crew members found these chores to be just busy work. Eventually the crew felt angered by the useless suggestions from earth. The Internet provided some relief however their mission was being discussed and mis-understood by many people.

"I guess there is going to be an interesting welcome when we get back. I am sure I am going to take all of the heat for Benjamin and Nanci staying on Mars. As the commander of the mission, is was my responsibility to bring them back. If anything happens to them I'm history." Stephen said in an exasperated tone.

"It wasn't your choice you could not force them to come along" answered Judy in an attempt to relieve

Mars Life

Stephen's guilt.

But the die had been cast, there were a million opinionated people waiting to hear the story. History would be made upon their return, however if the crew had any thoughts of riches beyond the dreams of avarice, they were now extinguished. The events were as the events were and only time would determine the ultimate outcome. As it turns out, the crew kept contact with the ground team once every few days; they seemed normal and happy to have pioneered the planet. The food supplies were slowly increasing, building structures was proving easy. Several sturdy structures had been manufactured from the local stone and dirt. Another well had been started to bring up water. Within a few years the ground team would be joined by more settlers, but for now they toiled everyday in an effort to stave off any risks from the local environment. They chose structures based on practicality and utility. These were rooms with thick walls to shield from solar radiation as well as keep heat and air in. There could be few windows based on the Plexiglas and plastic sheets that were left, these windows were on the lower portions of structures to protect the upper portions from leaks. It would take geologists a few years to locate silicon on the Martian surface to make more transparent windows. But for now a little paradise was being made that was comfortable and safe.

204

Mars Life

Back on the Thales, Stephen and Judy maintained a semblance of normalcy by having breakfast together. Initially these were silent affairs sans the discussions on the daily activities. At some point however, the discussions turned more philosophic, both crew members were well read and followed the discoveries from earth and space bound telescopes. On day 94, after the mundane discussions were over Stephen asked Judy about life in space.

"So Judy, besides us now, is there life in other worlds?", started Stephen.

"Probably," was the quick answer.

"Are you basing that on intuition?" continued Stephen.

"You know, I have though about this for a long time, our careers bring us close to the people who should know the most about these things. NASA, scientists, and other interested parties are all around us. We watch the astrophysical journals and other reputable publications and there seem to be several common threads about the subject. A great many people feel that there is life out there from an intuitional point of view. In other words, of the many billions of stars in the many billions of galaxies in the known universe, how could it be a statistical impossibility for other life not to exist? But there is no proof. SETI researchers and radio astronomers have searched a long time for signals, they keep hearing things but no one is convinced that these are intelligent messages from ET. These searches are usually on frequencies that would require an intelligent civilization with good technology and identical reasonings as us. In other words, they would have to transmit signals near 1,420 MHz to us or that frequency times pi other similarly reasoned places. Maybe they would us optical means instead of radio, maybe gamma radiation or cosmic rays......we assume they think like us and are of the same technical level as us. But life includes bugs and bees and algae. A planet made up of water and algae has life, just not the kind we can communicate with. And I think that the answer of extra-terrestrial life is more in defining the levels of life and their probable existence than assuming they are like us with four limbs and a radio transmitter. Our own arrogance wants them to look like us, or at least similar, like Star Trek many years ago. But look at how we got here, with dinosaurs reining the world until a stray asteroid hit us. Who is to say that we should have been intelligent reptiles instead of advanced tarsiers? We arrogantly assume that DNA is the only form of life and therefore must follow the rules of DNA evolution with similar environments. I don't know Stephen, but I think it is out there but more like trees and lizards. Most likely I am wrong considering all of the other possibilities. I think however, that whoever they are there will be some commonalities with us. Fundamentally, they will strive to exist just like us. They will adapt to changes as best they can to continue to exist. I think also, that if they become sentient they will have questions about themselves and their essence and produce answers to fill in the gaps. They will be social for protection and forced to have rules and mores to co-exist. Gender is possibly optional although probable. I say that based on examples of asexual reproduction examples on earth, like the hydra. At what point do they look skyward and wonder about other life in the universe? Again, it is our arrogance that assumes they even care. What if their world is constantly covered with clouds? The concept of life on other stars would be unknown until they ventured above the clouds, and only then could they start to explore the universe. You know, I really think that we are looking at the wrong signature for life, radio astronomers have the ability to look for chemical signatures on other worlds, why not concentrate on methane or carbon dioxide or combinations of chemicals that will lead us more scientifically to a conclusion of life elsewhere?"

"Actually," followed Stephen, "I always thought that if there was sentient life out there it would announce itself in the lowest part of the electromagnetic spectrum before moving upward. I say this only because that is the way we did it; and you are right, it is arrogant to assume they look or think like we do. But I would listen for emanations from the lower megahertz region before the higher. Our first transmitters put out energy in the Kilohertz, then Megahertz regions. Tesla and Marconi used low frequencies initially and added significant amounts of power before moving upward in the spectrum. Technically it was harder to produce signals at higher frequencies. It was also harder to de-modulate them. But can you image how much noise we make at 60 Hz. Not for communication but for the transmission of power. The earth is covered in transmitters and antennas radiating at 50 to 60 cycles per second. Although the ionosphere reflects much of this back to the ground there must be some portion of the gazillion megawatts of energy we produce at these frequencies that can escape. Even on Thales, the spectrum analyzers with small antennas can pick up the noise. I don't know, but I would look there before I would look at 20 GHz."

"Makes sense," completed Judy, "If there ever is a discovery about a sophisticated high frequency signal or device, I would be very concerned."

"Yeah and oh by the way, mission control is trying to figure out why you are not doing your chores," continued Judy.

"I'll get to them, its just busy work with no purpose,"

lamented Stephen.

"Yeah but it will keep you from going nuts," Judy said, releasing her belts at the table to move aft and start her own work.

Philosophic discussions were fun but they needed to keep doing things to make the time flow faster, they still had several weeks to go in the journey and plenty of time for Plato.

Plato indeed found his way into their daily conversations. For some reason it became easier to discuss philosophic issues floating way out in space instead of technical or political themes. They were instead a philosopher's dream, two minds separated from the noise and morass of human thought in the midst of large populations and massive sensory bombardment.. What better place to consider essence and existence but as just another twinkling star in the night sky? Reading Kant and Descartes lead to interesting discussions and many "logos" experiences, as Heidegger had described. Who is God, one asked during a particular early morning session. Right now, God is the oxygen re generator that keeps us alive was the capricious answer. We must worship that piece of equipment until we land. After that, we can consider other ideas.

With that philosophical discussion at an end,

Mars Life

Stephen and Judy went back to their routines. The boredom continued to grow day by day.

Chapter 2: Noise on the Radios

"Its over there, I see several greenhouses and structures"

On earth, NASA held discussions regarding the crews return. Several thousand hours were spent on how to handle public reaction. The two pioneer mars inhabitants became stuff of legends; even though they were still alive and in fact partially reachable through e-mail. When did they know they wanted to stay? Did NASA actually plan this secretly?   Would they ever come home?   The questions became endless with 24 hour dedicated chat lines overflowing with comments.

Meanwhile, during the excitement and speculation another issue was evolving. A small group of amateur radio astronomers based in Colorado had been scanning the skies with a government surplus 60 foot dish. Made up of scientists, engineers, physicists, ham radio operators and just generally interested individuals; this group had met over the years and found several uses for the old equipment. They followed balloon flights to the edge of space, they tracked satellites just launched by NASA and other groups to verify performance. They also placed simple radio receivers in the focus of this rather larger aperture.   The sensitivity of such a large dish allowed them to map the distribution of radio emissions in space,   like pulsars, supernova remnants and a host of other phenomena. The "observatory" as some called it was host to many school groups and clubs interested in astronomy.

Professional radio astronomers had long ago starting using superior technology and had no real interest in the archaic instrument.   It would be like asking optical astronomers to use 6" backyard telescopes to do real research.   There were just too many superior radio telescopes in the world to use.

Mars Life

The group named themselves the Deep Space Exploration Society and met once a month to discuss plans for operations and visitors. Although competent, the DSES activities where more in the form of an advanced hobby by highly intelligent individuals. Situated on a government owned mesa north of Boulder, Colorado. The facility actually consisted of two 60 foot parabolic dishes on pedestals. One was used for science and the other typically in the stowed position. A control room some 40 feet by 20 feet lay near the foot of the operational dish. Talented individuals from all walks of life spent hundreds of hours cleaning, painting, and refurbishing the electrical circuits to allow experiments to take place. In a way, this place was a kind of Mecca for like minded individuals wanting to explore the cosmos.

One night however, their coffee and donut discussions were interrupted by a serendipitous discovery.

The control room was set up with two separate areas, one for storage and meetings and the second smaller room housed the radio equipment. Most of this equipment was donated or made by the small group of researchers. Several computers ranging from 20 years old to 5 years old ran the programs to analyze the output of a homemade spectrometer. This spectrometer actually was not unlike a TV set with multiple channels. The difference was that the

213

channels were very close together and all centered around 21 cm or 1,420 MHz. This particular frequency was one of the most interesting frequencies insofar as it represented the presence of hydrogen. In fact, it also shows the movement of hydrogen by virtue of its Doppler shift. This particular evening the DSES group was mapping the presence of hydrogen in the arms of the Milky Way. For fun one of the members also had written a subroutine to sound an alarm for unusually strong signals.

The members sat, mostly talking about exciting developments in space science and their normal jobs.

Rex was the president of the group and had been there for over five years. He was a specialist in optics and worked at a local aerospace firm. He had led the group during the rebuilding process and had turned the facility into a reasonable place to do research. Thoughtful in nature, Rex respected everyone's opinion and when he offered his own, he was taken seriously. His opinion would invariably be well thought out with years of engineering experience to give it credibility. Peter, another member, was a distinguished member of the technical staff at a large telecom firm. His engineering expertise was first class and that coupled with his work ethic made him an indispensable member of the "observatory" staff. Peter was responsible for the hardware and software that steered the great instrument. His creations moved 36 tons of telescope to within small fractions of a degree even in the presence of high winds and changing temperatures. He along with another process engineer from a local brewery, had labored over many years to build up the necessary equipment to correctly position the behemoth. Gary a relative newcomer had been there for 2 years and was a software specialist. His efforts allowed the receivers to work properly and all digital information was fed to servers he designed to allow the remote use of the facility over the Internet. In addition, Gary had a good understanding of receivers and antennas that was also indispensable. These people along with the other 50 members, spent many hours cleaning and fixing and building things necessary to transform this once warehouse into a respectable research facility. All this and on a volunteer basis. It was a unique site and group of people and on this particular night, serendipity came to call.

"Bleep,Bleep,Bleep,Bleep,Bleep," sounded the internal pc buzzer. The same alarm that sounds when a file is done transferring. Not really loud, just noticeable.

"What's that?" asked Rex, getting up to look at the displays.

"Probably another interference alarm," answered Peter, "just like last week."

"Let's check it out and clear it," noted Gary, putting

down a cup of coffee to note the readings.

Gary walked over the the output computer, noted the signal strength and celestial position. This computer was showing graphs of the spectrometer output, generally a white line across a blue background. In the upper left was the right ascension and declination that the telescope was pointed at. In the upper right was the maximum and minimum values for the day. This particular measurement however showed a horizontal line with a few bumps with the exception of near the exact center where there existed a huge signal with multiple "side lobes" indicating a signal with modulation. This meant that the signal had information embedded in it. On earth it was illegal to transmit on this frequency due to its importance in the field of astronomy so the presence of any large, modulated signal was very unusual.

"Huh, check this out guys," said Gary. "This is not normal interference, its very close to center, just slightly positive, coming towards us."

The rest of the members came over to the display to look at the unusual signal. Normally, local interference showed itself as a simpler, off center signal with less intensity. These were caused by various transmitters that were not filtered properly, after a few years of looking at spectra, the DSES members could easily distinguish noise and bad transmitters from true signals. But this new signal was unusual on several accounts, it just did not belong where it was and certainly did not look right for local interference. To these observers, it was like a car driving on the wrong side of the street.

"That's bizarre," started Rex, "that just doesn't belong there. Lets move the dish to see if it goes away and warm up the test equipment to check the calibration of the receiver."

As Peter moved the big dish away from the source, the signal faded rapidly. He then moved the dish back to the newly found radio source and continued beyond to see the effects. The signal grew in intensity, peaked and then faded as the dish moved beyond the source's position in the sky.

"Looks sidereal," commented Gary. "Lets do a drift scan to verify."

Peter moved the great dish to point just ahead of the radio source so that the movement of the earth would allow the telescope "beam" to drift though the source. This technique allowed them to make a determination of whether or not the radio source was in the stars or a satellite in orbit around the earth.

After a few minutes, the source again peaked and faded indicating that in fact its position was fixed with the stars. This made it interesting. The source was way too "loud" for its position in the sky.

"Lets track and record it," said Rex.

"Ok, the equipment checks out and I will start the tape recorder," said Gary. "This is way too complicated for a local transmitter. Look at the change in modulation patterns. They are moving from amplitude modulation to frequency modulations to a type I have never seen before. This is absolutely amazing."

For five hours the group tracked and recorded the signal, as it grew later in the night the source continued to track with the stars and eventually, as the earth turned, the source became closer and closer to the Western horizon. Finally, is went below the horizon and the signal faded. The group was still stunned with the nature of the signal, definitely celestial in origin and with complicated modulation patterns that none of the members had ever seen before. They burned Cds of the signal's readings from the multi channel tape recorder and marked the signal's position on a star chart.

"Hey, this position puts it close to Mars," remarked Peter, "Maybe its the returning space ship Thales."

"I don't think so," commented Gary. "I have a tracking program from NASA that shows Thales a few degrees from the signal's center. Also, Thales does not have any transmitters on this frequency as far as I know and of course transmissions on this frequency are illegal."

"Rather curious that is either in line or close to Thales," noted Rex, "Lets track it tomorrow and check with the authorities if it still is as interesting as it was tonight. I am going to run some signal analysis software on the recordings to see if anything makes sense."

"LGP three," quipped Peter, referring to signal of unknown origin once observed several years ago from the same facility. LGP was an acronym for 'Little Green People' named after unexplained readings from other radio telescopes over the years. LGP two had gotten several people excited three years ago when another observatory in Holland observed the same strange emanation from the constellation Ursa Major. Their astronomers had flown to the Very Large Array immediately to use a superior instrument to try to examine the signal further. The signal lasted for several days and was in the 400 MHz region, not observable by the world class array. However, the astronomers learned of the work of the DSES and felt that due to the coincidental siting, the source was reputable. Because of the short duration however, the source was never observed again.

Tonight's signal brought back that spine tingling feeling everyone felt during the LGP2 experience.

Mars Life

Something was there, now the group had to do everything possible to explain it away as something man made or natural in origin. This task proved to be very difficult.

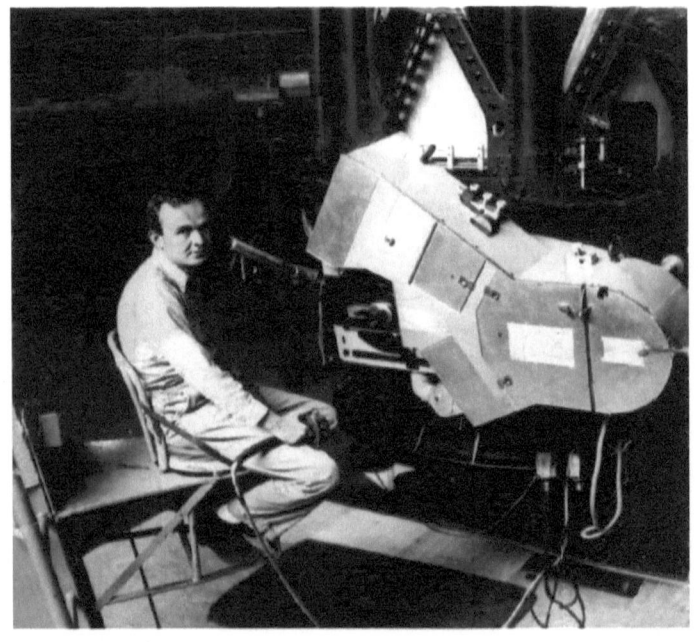

Chapter 3: Verification and Rationalizing

"Don your suits, lets go for a visit"

"I just got an interesting call," said Eliot, (a professional astronomer from a university in Arizona). "Calls about celestial siting come in almost once a week from backyard astronomers as well as crazy people," he continued, talking to a graduate student. "But this one was

221

a little more interesting. These guys rebuilt an old government facility and seem to be pretty competent. They just found an interesting radio source near Mars with unusual modulation. They are checking with Norad and NASA today to find out if there is anything man made out there. But the source tracks sidereally, with the stars. That counts satellites out. Its probably a local ham radio operator making noise with a lousy radio design, but I was intrigued by the fact that they are pretty serious observers with a lot of experience. They gave me a position in RA and Dec (Right Ascension and Declination), lets put the 14" on it tonight and check it for them. I don't think these guys are your standard goof balls seeing things after a case of Coors."

The graduate student took note of the location and made plans to use one of the smaller telescopes at the observatory. The other, larger ones were in use looking at variable stars and supernovas. Maybe with a good night sans clouds, he would see something.

Jason, the graduate student, prepared the telescope starting at dusk. He would use a very sensitive electronic camera first and track the exact location. If there was nothing observable, he would look around the immediate area. He decided to spend a decent amount of time to examine that area of the sky. As a graduate student, he did not want to disappoint his professor, especially Eliot who had a world wide reputation. Although Jason had in fact fielded calls from people seeing flying saucers, this was a different story.

The equipment was made ready and when the source started to rise from the horizon, Jason commanded the telescope to start tracking the area of interest. Insofar as it was still just after dusk, Jason decided to go get a cup of coffee and return to start the search.

As he was returning from the cafeteria, Jason ran into a friend of his from one of his classes, Audrene.

"Hey, how are you doing," she asked "what's up tonight?"

"Oh I don't know yet, something mysterious," answered Jason. "Eliot asked my to try to find a source of radio emission near Mars. It was discovered by some amateurs North of Boulder, probably nothing but we'll see," continued Jason.

"So what if it really is something?" asked Audrene. "What if its intelligent? Do you guys ever talk about that?"

"That stuff is for philosophers and mystics," said Jason, "we do research, not Oiji boards."

"Yeah but someday life will be discovered out there, I think," continued Audrene, "what are you pros going to do then?"

"You know," answered Jason "life *is* probably going

to be discovered out there, probably by us 'pros', and it will be algae or fungus or maybe even vegetation. But intelligent life trying to communicating with us requires a whole bunch of things to go right at the same time. That is going to take a long long time in my opinion."

"Aw, common be an optimist," chided Audrene "maybe tonight is the night."

"Actually tonight is the night for me to be competent in the eyes of my professor, I need to graduate someday," said Jason opening up the door to the main hallway to return to the telescope, "see you later, OK?"

Audrene left for the library as Jason worked his way through the astronomy department to the waiting telescope.

Working his way down cream colored hallways lit by fluorescent lights, Jason walked the same floor as countless other astronomers and astronomy students. All looking forward to discoveries, of which there are so many to be found in the universe. Some of these people contributed much in the science of astronomy, even by just measuring stars' positions, or examining spectroscopic details to find planets or companion stars. Some of the most mundane boring work in astronomy had produced great discoveries. For instance, Cycilia Payne Kapushkin spent years looking at photographic plates and cataloging brightness changes amongst thousands of stars. Her work was rewarded by the discovery that periodic changes in some stars types of stars (LL Lyrae) are an indication of the distance to these stars even though they could be in other galaxies. After her work, the known universe simply doubled in size. Not bad for one person. Jason was on track to discovery as well, his interests were in interferometric optics. These techniques were used to increase the resolving power of telescopes by connecting two or more reflectors in such a away as to combine their light into one image. This was not a trivial task, however the rewards were great because the distance between the two telescopes as projected on the sky dictated the resolving power. This meant that researchers could could potentially synthesize telescopes a hundred plus meters in diameter. Impossible to build physically, these combination telescopes or optical interferometers could detect planets around other stars and greatly enhance the knowledge of our own solar system.

Jason would be working on this research for his doctorate, but tonight a slight detour was needed. Moving down the hallway to the door that leads to the observatory control room, he pondered the likely hood that anything of interest would be found this night. Usually he guessed a 2% chance of anything worth noting during these forays. Tonight would be a repeat except for the fact that Eliot, his adviser had been unusually excited about this.

Mars Life

He walked up the stairs to a dimly lit room with several computers in it with large displays. The room smelled like electronics, like ozone and dust combined. It sounded like electronics as well due to the multitude of cooling fans to keep the equipment from melting. The faster the computer, the hotter it gets and this room was hot. Of the six monitors lined up on a table, only one was showing the image from the telescope Jason was using tonight. The other displays were for tracking and housekeeping information. There was also a planetarium program running on one of the monitors to guide the researchers to their images of interest.

Jason sat down to get to work, first he used the planetarium program to find Mars and noted that it would be rising above the Eastern horizon in about 30 minutes. This gave him time to open the observatory dome and calibrate the telescope. Pushing various buttons, the doors opened and the instrument swung around to get ready to observe the red planet. He set out a schedule to observe the planetary disk initially followed by the surrounding space to look for anything anomalous. "90% perspiration and 10% inspiration," he mused, thinking of Einstein. "Actually tonight will just be perspiration."

Mars, the object of a million observations and almost as many theories, rose as predicted and the telescope started to automatically track its movement across the sky. Jason waited for the planet to move 15 degrees above the horizon (which took an hour) before he started taking data. First images for calibration of the focus system and imaging electronics. Next he prepared the computer to file the images in a particular directory. Last he inputed his scanning plan to the tracking computer. As the telescope moved around the area near Mars, it paused to take images for later examination. The whole process was automatic and all Jason had to do was make sure the computers did their work. Hour after hour passed as the telescope slewed to new coordinates and paused. Star field after star field appeared on the image monitor with nothing interesting to note. Several more hours past, Jason got up for another cup of coffee, wandered around a bit in the room and made his way back to the observer's station. A point of light flashed on the image monitor a few degrees away from the planet's position.

"Probably a satellite's glint," thought Jason. But just for fun Jason commanded the telescope to remain in that area of the sky just for confirmation. Another flash, some 10 seconds later. The flash seemed to last about 2 seconds. This was a little longer that the satellite glints he had seen before. He continued to watch and another 10 seconds later, another 2 second flash. Curious, he centered the scope on the flash area and zoomed in a bit to see if there was any movement in the flash source. Again, 10 second later another two second flash. This time the larger image showed a striated pattern indicative of some variations on the light's amplitude. Jason, noted also that the source of the light was either moving very slowly or not at all, unlike a satellite at this declination.

"This isn't a man-made object," thought Jason. Again another flash. "And its staying on time same position in the sky. Lets look a little closer my friend," Jason caught himself talking to himself, stopped and pushed a few buttons to start high speed recordings of the images. He also zoomed in a little further. Again another flash. With the high speed recording equipment on, he waited until after another flash to examine the images in slow motion. There was no doubt about the fact that the light was changing in brilliance with an unnatural pattern. The pattern repeated every 10 seconds but was clearly complex like Morse code. Jason took more high speed images and found that there were 256 light pulses with a binary like pattern that made up the two second burst. After a few seemingly quick hours later, Mars was starting to set and the Sun was about the rise. The night had gone quickly. Jason by now was getting excited about the light source. It was flashing a continuous repeatable sequence of pulses. It was stationary in a part of the sky where no satellite could be stationary and was coincident with the position from the radio astronomers. The spectra of the light was also unusual. He need more data the next night, but for now it was time to tell Eliot.

Shaking and tired, Jason gathered the data on a disk and made his way to Eliot's office. The first classes were starting with sleepy students and professors. Jason however was wide awake and eager to show the results to his professor. The office was closed however he noted that Eliot was due to teach a class at 8:30. Jason hopped that Eliot would stop by his office before class and parked himself on the floor across from the office door. 45 minutes elapsed when Eliot came down the hallway.

"I found something amazing," Jason said in a loud voice as he sprang to his feet and walked toward the professor. "Your not going believe this, there was an object near the coordinates you gave me, it pulses a modulated signal every 10 seconds. The signal has an embedded......"

"Whoa, there fireball," interjected Eliot, "slow down and tell me in English."

"The coordinates you gave me, from the radio astronomers North of Boulder, I moved the 14 inch telescope and tracked that area with a spiral scan last night, I found nothing for 6 hours, then a flash, this one (holding up an plot of stars with a bright dot near the center), this one doesn't belong here, its not a star, its not a star at all," gasped Jason.

"Ok, Ok come in my office, quiet down and while I teach class I want you to call the following people and ask for confirmation." commanded Eliot. "Mars is visible in Australia now, call George Dulk at this number, tell him to look and confirm. Don't tell him all of the details yet, just ask for confirmation. Also, call this guy at Norad in Colorado Springs, make sure it is not space junk."

"Its not, it can't be, it wouldn't," interjected Jason.

Eliot interrupted and said, "look, calm down and do the right thing; cross the t's and dot the i's. Don't leave any room for us to be embarrassed tomorrow by the discovery that it was a high altitude balloon or something."

Jason sat down as Eliot left for class and made the first phone call to Australia. Dr. Dulk answered and realizing who asked for the confirmation quickly commanded his observatory to move to the coordinates. He told Jason that he would call back if he found anything. The next call was to Norad, the tenor of the conversation was much different. "You know, there are 15,000 pieces of space junk up there, I am sure it is one of them; we'll check and get back to you," said the lieutenant at the operations desk.

Jason waited for a few minutes, decided he was

hungry and needed to get some food. He rose to look for a vending machine when the phone rang. He did not expect any answers for many hours so he assumed that it was a student or family member on the line.

"Astrophysics department," he answered.

"Jason, this is George, we have a positive hit on your object, pretty bright, magnitude 5, same coordinates, this thing has a modulation pattern I have never seen before. I am sending you an e-mail with a movie file attached, tell Eliot, if he found something interesting, I want to support him 100%."

"Thank you Dr. Dulk, thank you, I will tell Eliot right after class," stammered Jason.

Jason got up again, conscious of the fact that his stomach was getting angry, probably due to the excitement and lack of food. The phone rang again and Jason went back to the desk to answer.

"Astrophysics department," he answered.

"Jason this is lieutenant Smith at Norad, we don't have any radar returns or infrared images from that area. We suggest you continue to monitor it in case it is something we need to get involved in. If you see it a few more times, we will need a complete report, OK?"

"Ok, we will look for it again tonight and report if it is still there however we just got an initial confirmation from an observatory in Australia," answered Jason.

"If you see it again tonight we will put a telescope on it as well," continued the lieutenant, let us know."

Jason acknowledged and hung the phone up. Now his stomach was really getting angry. He rose, went to the door, stopped to look at the phone once more and went down the hall for food and to find Eliot again. With shaking hands he obtained a bag of cookies and went down the hallway to the lecture classes. Soon he heard the voice of Eliot talking about stellar distances in a classroom. Jason went to the doorway, out of sight of the students inside and waited for Eliot to see him standing in the hallway. Eliot was drawing figures on the white board and talking but soon paused to turn around towards his students. As he did so, he noticed Jason in the doorway holding a bag of cookies and staring, unblinking at him. Eliot paused to acknowledge Jason's presence. Jason quickly gave Eliot a thumbs up sign which made Eliot stop, excuse himself from class and approached Jason.

"Dr. Dulk confirmed, he wants to continue watching it tomorrow, Norad says nothing is there but if we see something again, they want to know about it and will put a scope on it as well, Eliot we're in trouble," stammered Jason.

"Nonsense Jason, this is where the fun begins,"

comforted Eliot. "Go home and get some rest, come back before Mars rises again and I will work with you tonight."

Jason left the building to go home and try to get some sleep. He laid in bed for hours, too excited to sleep until late in the afternoon. Soon after dropping off, the alarm sounded to wake him. Groggy, Jason got up and within minutes remembered the importance of the previous night. He quickly dressed and grabbing a sandwich left the house where he lived and returned back to the observatory. As luck would have it Audrene was returning home from classes and they happened to pass each other.

"Well, did you find ET?" asked Audrene.

"Worse, something really weird, and we got confirmation," said Jason, "Eliot is on it tonight, it could be big, I will tell you more later." He quickly walked away with Audrene saying, "Just remember the little people!"

He made it back to the control room to find Eliot and several other professors waiting. Mars would be up in another hour and the aura of something important had infected the astronomy staff.

"Come in and close the door," commanded the chairman of the department with a sober look on his face.

Jason followed his orders and sat down.

"Something is a-foot son, when Eliot stays at work late and his graduate student looks like he was just shot out

233

of a canon. Why don't you let us know what is going on," queried the chairman.

A Bach prelude played on the FM radio faintly in the background, one of the attending professors reached to the radio and turned it off, leaving a pregnant silence.

Jason sat down at a long table and along with Eliot, explained the discovery of the modulated light source near Mars. As they spoke about the details of the light source, the largest scope in the observatory was brought to bear on the coordinates from the previous night.

The professors asked a myriad of questions and formed their own opinions about the subject, arguing about whether or not it was artificial or some sort of natural phenomena. As their theories evolved, the light source rose above the eastern horizon to be viewed by the professors. All of the bantering and arguing ceased when the light was seen for the first time with a bigger scope and better equipment. Measurements and recordings was made and for once in a very long time, the professors and Jason worked together as a team as apposed to a mentor and apprentice, each contributing to the formation of a cogent explanation of the light. No one was jealously guarding secrets for first publication, the discovery was too big for that. Within hours, they had all concluded that the source was indeed artificial, was sending modulated signals in a way no one had seen before and was positioned somewhere between Mars and Earth, moving slowly against the backdrop of stars.

"In a few days we can determine the parallax of the object and determine its position," mentioned Eliot.

"Or how about simultaneously observing the source with two telescopes at opposite sides of the earth?" asked Jason

"Might work," theorized the chairman, "you might graduate after all Jason!"

A plan formed to have Dr. Dulk photograph the object at the same time as Jason and Eliot, then the images would be compared to determine the relative angle of observation relative to the background of stars. These angles would allow a better determination of the object's parallax and thus the position and range. Dr. Dulk was advised and brought into the confidence of the group, the discovery could be big enough for all of them.

One of the professors was a ham radio operator and decided to try to decode the fast light pulses. After about an hour he announced that the pulses were indeed a series of binary number counting from 1 to 256 with great regularity, as accurately as the observatory clocks could measure. Also, the light appeared to have unique spectral qualities, showing patterns of colors while they counted.

These color patterns held a more difficult code to interpret and the professor, Mark, continued to work on the problem.

"By the way," mused the chairman late in the evening, "where is the Mars return ship now? It certainly is in the area, they have some decent scopes on board, maybe we should find out it they can see it."

All present agreed it was a good idea, but within a few seconds a wave of anxiety moved over the group. It became obvious to everyone that there was a potential danger. They had determined that the source was somewhere in a line between the Earth and Mars and was not man made. With new found energy they decided to call Dr. Dulk immediately, bring him into the fold and get images as soon as possible from Australia. The called as dusk was falling near Perth and within minutes had Dr. Dulk driving to his observatory. As it was getting to be light the group of professors decided to cancel classes or find substitutes, get some sleep and then devote all of their energies into determining exactly where the light source was.

Meanwhile the radio astronomers in Colorado had not heard anything from Eliot. The three principles sent a series of e-mails back and forth the discuss the lack of communications from

"Your buddy blew you off," chided Gary, "have you talked to him recently?"

"This makes me nervous, either they figured out where out of our minds or something real is happening," continued Peter.

"I will e-mail them to find out if anything has been done, seems a little strange that we haven't heard anything," followed Rex.

The next day, Eliot and his team waited for results from Australia, and in a moment of boredom, he went to his computer to check on the outside world.

"Rats, I forgot to call this guy," as Eliot read a very polite e-mail asking for further information on the source. He e-mailed back to call immediately on his cell phone, then left a number. In all of the excitement, little consideration was given to the fact that the source was also sending information over radio waves.

Within the hour, Eliot's cell phone rang with Rex on the other end.

"Did you guys find anything? I realize you are busy and probably have better things to do but......," asked Rex.

"Yeah, we found something and its big, the thing you detected has a very complex optical pattern starting with binary counting but with interlaced variations in color. It was right where you told us, now we are trying to locate its precise position. All we know know is that it appears to be between Mars and Earth and as you know, so is the Mars return craft with several people on board. We are waiting for an image from Australia to better determine its position and then we need to go to NASA if its close to the space craft. This is big Rex, how soon can you and your people get here?" Eliot said with a definite tone of urgency.

"Jeez, let me get hold of our people and tell them what happened," stammered Rex, "how soon do you need us there."

"Now, right now, get on a plane, get all of your data and get on a plane," said Eliot.

"Ok, I will call you back, my goodness I..., ok we'll be there soon," responded Rex.

Phones rang in several offices in Colorado followed by a second round to the associated wives, followed by one back to Eliot.

"We land at nine pm your time, we pawned our cars to get the plane tickets so soon," Rex said to Eliot.

"If this is what we think it is, you won't have any problem paying the pawn shops. Someone will meet you at the airport. We are a wreck here, the first image came back from Australia and it appears this object is very close the the Mars return ship. Get here as soon as possible, when you arrive we will conference with NASA and that's probably when all hell will break loose, be prepared. Call me as soon as you get here," Eliot said with a serious tone.

238

Rex hung up the phone and again called Gary and Peter, "I don't know exactly whats going on but they are serious, we are going to talk to NASA tonight about the proximity of this object to the return ship from Mars, see you all at the airport."

****

Meanwhile on the spaceship Thales:

"Did you eat the stroganoff? I was saving that for later," asked Stephen.

"That stroganoff wasn't yours Stephen, I can eat whatever I want, and quit being a jerk, its hard enough keeping occupied without you pontificating around here all the time," responded Nanci.

"I am the commander here and if I want........................"

"Thales this is ground control with an urgent message.....Thales this is ground control with an urgent message, do you copy?"

The message was broadcast over the entire ship and stopped Stephen and Nanci cold. This was the most urgent sounding call they had received.

"This is Thales, go ahead ground control," responded Stephen.

"Thales, we have an urgent message from you from the administrator, stand by one."

The Thales crew waited for a few seconds and then..

"Thales this is NASA Director Smith, we have a problem, or more importantly you have a problem. We have received confirming evidence that an object or ship is in your general vicinity. This object is of unknown origin and is transmitting coded messages on optical and radio frequencies. We are now downloading positional information to your computers and advise you to immediately start monitoring the spectrum analyzers on board for signals as well as turn your on board telescopes to the designated coordinates. It is imperative that you do this immediately. Do you copy?"

"We copy ground, Nanci is making her way to the control panels and we will advise when we find it, Thales out," said Stephen.

Nanci had propelled herself down the hallway in the craft at such a rate that she crashed into a bulkhead before reaching her destination. Bruised, she continued to move quickly to the control station for the telescopes and spectrum analyzers. The up link data was streaming in and the displays showed coordinates relative to the ship. She commanded the main observational telescope to move to

240

the correct azimuth and elevation. Meanwhile Stephen had arrived to take over the spectrum analyzers.

"I'm getting close to the position. The up link data says this thing is getting closer to us, hope its friendly," said Nanci.

"Me too," responded Stephen, "the equipment is warming up so I should find something soon."

"I have something," Nanci said with an elevated tone. "I am switching to track mode. It definitely is changing brightness, colors too, its definitely there Stephen, let them know."

"I see it too, radiating on a wide frequency band, very clear," stammered Stephen. He plugged in the headset to advise ground control.

"Ground Control this is Thales."

"Thales this is ground, go ahead."

"Ground, we have it, tracking it now, it is radiating on a wide frequency band and is changing colors optically, can you tell us how close it is?" asked Stephen.

"Thales we are tracking it with everything we have now, it is moving toward your position and is altering its course to match yours. Right now it does not appear to be a threat, but it does have some intelligence. Monitor it carefully, initiate your maneuvering systems and prepare Thales to move away if necessary. We have our best people on it and will advise you of any changes. Down link all of your data."

"Roger that ground, we will power up Thales and prepare to move if it looks like a problem," responded Stephen.

He went up to the cockpit and started the necessary systems to enable a course change. Meanwhile, Nanci monitored the position of the object and made enough measurements to realize that the craft was slowing to a parking position a discrete distance away from Thales, but definitely parallel in course.

"Stephen, the object is paralleling our course now at 500 meters. It is still sending signal out in both optical and radio frequencies. I have a radar on it now and its holding its distance to within millimeters."

"Ok Nanci, I will advise ground and I want you to prepare for some course changes here, you need to put your flight suit on with your helmet close by, we can't take any chances," commanded Stephen.

"Got it, I will get prepared, what about securing the rest of the cabin?" asked Nanci.

"Forget it for now, we might not have any time, we might have to move quickly if this thing gets any closer, what is it doing now?" asked Stephen.

"Nothing, its just parked there, very precisely, no

changes," responded Nanci.

Stephen prepared the flight director and autopilot to move away from the unknown object with a single command. He then wired a remote switch to issue the command from anywhere in Thales. Once secure, he went back to the science stations where Nanci was to help in analyzing the thing.

"We're all set, one twitch from that thing and we are outta here," announced Stephen. He sat down at one of the observing positions and started to look at the radio and light emissions coming from the object. The binary counting sequence was obvious, as was the changes in color. But looking further is seemed that the object was also sending variations in hues and tints.

"Lets plot this thing," said Stephen. "Lets plot the color changes over time and see if there is any pattern. We should do the same with the tints".

Over the next few hours they tried several techniques to build an image from the data. By assigning numbers to colors in order of their radiating frequency and after discovering that the sequences of light where separated in time by a pause after every 1024 elements, recognizable patterns by scanning onto a x,y grid started to appear. After a while a crude image appeared, the top half was humanoid in appearance and the bottom half was like a movie of various scenes, symbols, landscapes and drawings. They telemetered the results to ground control to have their experts look at it, but it was becoming clear that there was an intelligence here and it was trying to communicate. The humanoid figure was upright walking with a head and arms, just like the imaginations of science fiction buffs of the 20th century. The movies were more interesting, they appeared to show daily life and history of the makers of the satellite. Stephen sent this data back to earth as well to let the anthropologists and other interested people dissect the information. The movies appeared to repeat every several hours, there was obviously a story to tell. He would let the experts handle it, for now Stephen's preoccupation was with the safety of the ship.

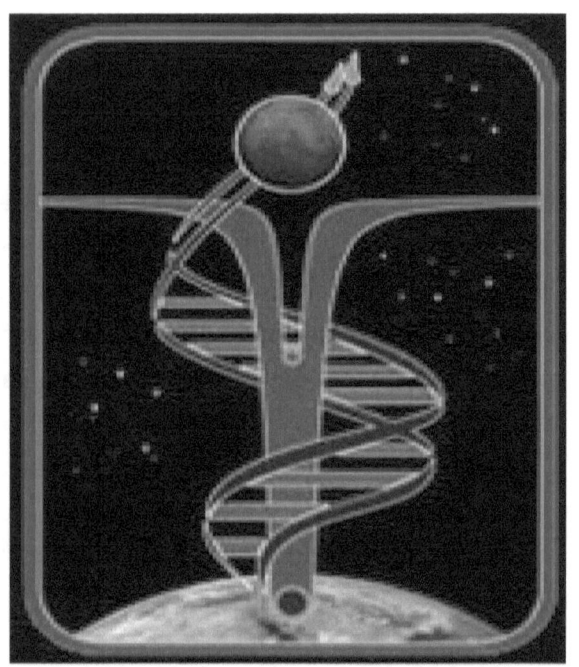

Chapter 6: A story emerges

"Open the hatch, we have them on the radio"

On earth, the astronomers, NASA personnel and other researchers went over the measurements and images. Within a few days a surprising story emerged, linguists had reviewed the symbols and movie fragments and come to the conclusion that the civilization that sent the satellite was indeed trying to make contact and in fact further analysis revealed that was probably sending back signals to its home world telling of its own discovery. The makers of the probe were from a nearby star group in Cygnus. They were as developed as our own species but with several minor differences and one major one. It was discovered that this species lived for only five earth years. They attained puberty at two years, middle age at four and were gone after five. This had the effect of shaping the mores of the society in such a way that it was extremely important for each individual to make one contribution to society no matter how small. Their engineers could only work on one project during their brief lifetime, the smartest individuals of the species designed the ultimate goals for their society, then broke down the pieces into manageable sizes. As a consequence, this idea of discovering new species in the local star group was the main effort for the culture and had taken many generations to accomplish. The intensity of focus this culture showed astonished the earth based anthropologists and sociologists. It became an point of introspection for most of the human race who lived so long comparatively and never needed to concentrate on just one task.

Mars Life

During the first days, Stephen and other people found out that the probe had in fact realized an intelligent species was examining it. It knew this because of the radar examinations and the light and radio emissions of the Mars return vessel. The probe did send back signal to its origin but in an almost undetectable way, using x-rays. The probe also allowed its examiners to see a "menu" of options to its own library. One of the options led the earth researchers to believe that a warning was attached.

It appeared in essence to say "do not attempt to capture me". Considering the great interest in the problem, this was going to be a hard rule to follow. Most of the earth bound researchers wanted to physically examine the satellite.

Another discovery in the memory banks of the probe indicated that the builders had compatible DNA. The size and shape of the aliens were similar to humans as well as many representations of their organs. There was also a numeric description of their genome.

But for now NASA was more interested in the actions of the probe and was letting the learned scientists from around the world examine the contents of its memory banks. The probe was definitely sending signals back to "home" somewhere in Cygnus. By examining the width of the beam emanating from the antenna, researchers could find the general area of the probe's origin. Several great observatories including the Hubble were sent to look for a likely candidate star system. Even infrared and radio telescopes were directed to examine the area of space that the probe was sending signals to. After a modicum of debate, the astronomers on earth decided that the star of origin was 33 Cygni. This star was about 3.6 times the size of our sun and about 152 light years away. The obvious implication was that the probe had been in space for a very long time, even if it was moving at near the speed of light. Considering the five year life span of the builders, many generations had passed since its launching. Was the earth the first civilization the probe encountered? There were few stars between 33 Cygni and our solar system, if it had visited others the en route the travel time would be even greater. Now a signal was propagating back at again the speed of light and so the inhabitants of their planet would not know of their discovery for another 152 light years. The earthly scientists were astounded at the patience and sincerity of purpose these aliens showed.

The scientists now considered what should be sent to the probe to relay to its masters. Initially, the greetings sent along with the Pioneer and Voyager probes were sent, but considering the "bandwidth" of the probe's transmissions a few symbols like those on our satellites would take a fraction of a second to transmit. The decision was to replicate what the probe was sending us and augment as necessary. For this purpose a large program was initiated at NASA to make up our story. It was designed like the probe's and sent via microwaves through Thales. There was no reaction from the probe and it was assumed that the probe was taking it all in. It was also assumed that in another 152 years, the architect's of the probe would learn of our existence. This large program was a culmination of many disciplines presenting their version of the "state of the art". Across the world, scientists, philosophers, theologians, politicians, medical practitioners and the general population submitted ideas and literature to best describe earth's inhabitants. Of course, arguments ensued at every opportunity where certain groups wanted more of their information relayed to the satellite. It took many meetings and the insights of many brilliant people to finally decide on how to handle the melange of information. All disciplines would be included and scholars from all educational institutions would present a synopsis of all written works much like an encyclopedia. The follow on information would be the first level of discoveries or achievements followed by other deeper levels of detail. They assumed that the "story" could be told first as a synopsis of the details to follow. They also assumed that the bandwidth was essentially

Mars Life

infinite and that the probe would transmit all of the information sent to it. In all, 4200 Terra-bytes of information was presented to the uplink specialists for transmission. As new discoveries and advancements were made, they too would be up-linked to the probe.

The center frequency of the probe's receiver was determined and the terra-bytes of information uploaded. This took several weeks, following the transmission, updates were sent every 24 hours. In this way it was hoped that the receivers of this information could get a snapshot of humanity as well as a measure of our growth rate. The probe was seen to relay the information as sent, and in 152 years of so, we would get a response to our story.

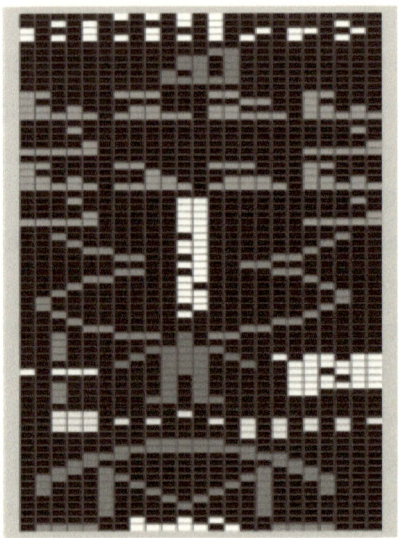

Chapter 7: Unity

"They will meet us on the other side of the pressure chamber"

The "Spheronts", as they called themselves had an amazing effect on earth's humanity. There was a great re-definition of the concept of "them" and "us". We were all of earth as distinct from the others, who where defined as not from earth. The hopes of great peace minded thinkers were starting to be realized. The concept of God had to be examined; was it the same God as the Spheronts' ? Did they in fact have a God? After due course, it was discovered that they indeed had religion with a few interesting parallels to most of Earths'; their religion has similar spiritual analogs; all events have purpose; unexplained events have origins. There were also central figures in their religions.

What about the stories, allegories, mores, ethics and moral compasses derived from our religious thought, were they the same as the Spheronts? The debates were long and furious. The resultant ethno centrism brought our civilization closer together than ever before and made us consider our similarities more that our differences.

But were they dangerous, would they eat us? Common ridiculous questions arose derived from fear as well as curiosity. In the end, fear and curiosity created the new battleground. The solution to the debates was to agree on who we thought the Spheronts were, then attempt to contact them and start a dialog. Of course the nature of the dialog was in question but no one disagreed of the fact that isolationism would not solve our new problems. Again, the scholars, politicians and scientists got together and decided on the best public policy. We would send a probe to the Spheronts home world with something important of ours, an invitation.

The new Terans as we now called ourselves began setting up dedicated radio and optical telescopes to monitor the Spheront home world. Every bit of information that was derived from the new comer of space was presented at yearly conferences on exo-biology and extra-terrestrial intelligence. The professional SETI people found themselves transformed from dreamers to practitioners overnight.

Chapter 7: Landing

"We are honored to meet you and bring best wishes from Earth"

The crew of the Thales went from heroes to unfortunate bystanders having witnessed a change in Earthling's perspectives due to the probe. There were admired for their journey of course in terms of their courage and discoveries but after the landing, work on the new world order would be waiting and they simply would just get back to work. Stephen and Nanci discussed the changes but were very much interested in getting home to view it for themselves. The changes upon their return were expected to be stark, only now it would be more so. At the beginning of the reentry procedure the ship moved away from the probe and was un-pursued. After several hours the probe remained in place near earth, how long it was going to remain there was anyone's guess.

Preparations upon the ship were made quietly and at a steady pace. Gear was stowed, fluids shifted to achieve the correct center of gravity. All system were checked and re-checked to assure a safe re-entry. It was determined that the ablative coating on the underside of the ship was in good shape and a full landing could take place. The plan was to slow the ship down to a virtual stop and let gravity take effect. The attitude would be controlled by reaction jets and, once in the atmosphere, by the aerodynamic surfaces (rudder, elevator and ailerons). Normally, vehicles that re-entered the earth's atmosphere came in at very specific angles and at great velocities. Work on the X-15 and Star Ship 1 projects proved that a slower landing profile would work and require less heat shielding. The 747 had thin tiles and special paint applied to its under side. Also it contained leading edge coolant systems to manage the heat generated by the re-entry. Heat sensors feed their measurements into the main computer for inclusion into the landing sub-routines. These measurements had significant "weight" in the determination of approach angles and speeds. The whole approach would be handled automatically, including the flight profile to 50,000 feet where all normal aerodynamic control laws would apply.

"Fuel transferred laterally."

"Check."

"Propellant transferred to high pressure tanks, main fuel pump on stand by."

"Check."

"Attitude stabilized and verified, computer has got a green light."

"Check."

"Transponder on, VHF radios set, flight director engaged."

"Check."

Stephen continued, "We are coming on the re-entry point, check your suit oxygen and all the emergency systems one more time."

Nanci replied; "Check...here we go and what a trip that was."

"Roger that."

The great aircraft gracefully rotated to present its tail to the direction of flight. Within seconds of achieving the optimal position the rocket engine that had propelled them into space once again fired and with reaction jets firing as well, slowed the ship to a standstill 300,000 feet above Cape Canaveral, Florida. The main engine ceased firing and the smaller reaction jets pushed the craft to present its belly to the beach filled with sun bathers and swimmers. Vertical descent commenced and built velocity quickly. Once an optimum downward speed was achieved, the nose of the craft lowered to initiate forward velocity. Although not flying yet, as the craft plunged through 200,000 feet, buffeting could be felt, telling the crew that air was near. The nose pitched over and the long inactive airspeed indicators started to fluctuate along with the electronic equipment standard for regular flight.

"We have Cape VOR and DME."

"Good."

"Skin temperature within limits, we are right on profile."

"Check."

"Turning to out bound course, coming through 100,000 feet."

"Check."

With that announcement came the knowledge that most risks of the re-entry were behind them. Soon the aircraft would be flying again and the crew would have to experience gravity and a change of roles, now they were

257

pilots not astronauts. The aircraft's nose continued to adjust to slowly bring up the airspeed to an indicated 270 knots. This would be locked in until the computer transitioned the flight director from space to air mode. The flight surfaces were becoming active again.

"We are still on profile passing through 70,000 feet, 240 knots indicated."

"Roger that."

"Coming up on 60,000 speed 255."

"Check"

"Flight surfaces in command mode, passing flight level 550, speed good, temperature good, engine two spooling up."

"Check, hydraulic pumps on, APU on, generators on."

"N1 above 25%, fuel switch on."

"Number two is running, starting number three."

"Roger."

"Ok, we have thrust on number two, three spooling up, fuel switch on."

"Looks good."

"Thrust on both engines"

"Airspeed stabilizing, computer in air mode, autopilots engaged, starting number one."

"Roger."

Mars Life

The 747 was now flying for the first time in many months. The engines were operating perfectly and as number one and number four came on line, the sound and feel of real flight overcame the crew. The commander adjusted a control to allow fresh air into the cabin.

"I can hear and smell the air."

"Nice isn't it?"

Flying level at flight level 500, the aircraft systems were checked and verified, leading to a conversation with air traffic control.

"Cape approach, this is Thales, level flight level five zero zero, heading one ten, speed two seventy indicated."

"Welcome home people, nice to hear you, we have full telemetry, all of your systems are nominal."

"Nice to be home, thanks."

"Thales, squawk five five one zero, descend and maintain one seven thousand."

"Five five one zero on the squawk, out of five zero zero for one seven thousand, Thales."

"Thales, right turn, heading one five zero."

"Right turn to one five zero, Thales."

The aircraft banked and descended with all of the gauges in the green, no different than a flight from Dallas the aircraft and crew followed a standard approach procedure to line up on the instrument landing system at

Cape Canaveral.

"Thales, descend to one zero thousand, right turn to three zero zero."

"Out of one seven thousand for one zero zero thousand, right to three zero zero, Thales."

"And Thales, slow to one eight zero, intercept the localizer."

"Slowing to one eight zero, intercept the localizer, Thales."

The captain commanded gear down and Judy lowered the lever to open up the gear doors and lower the massive wheels. There was some apprehension during this maneuver considering how long the gear had been stowed. The sound of rushing air and the distant "thunk" reassured the crew that the mechanisms still worked.

"Gear down and locked," reported Judy. "And listen to that air!"

"Ok," acknowledged Stephen, "read out the airspeed for me please."

"Roger that, we're coming up on the middle marker, landing check list complete,"

"Boots on and laced," thought Stephen referring to gear down and locked.

"160," reported Judy.

Now for some reason, Stephen thought about the

complete mission, all of its complexities, dangers and decisions. How would it look, how did it feel?

"150,"

Was it done correctly? What's going to happen now? The great adventure is over in 22 seconds. Stephen thought about advancing the throttles and going back to Mars, which as a result of his daydreaming caused the whine of the engines to change pitch a tiny bit, alerting Judy and making her sit up in her seat.

"145, over the fence speed, make me proud," Judy said with a smile.

"I haven't flown in a long while so forgive me is I turn it in to an arrival instead of a landing," replied Stephen. The crew became relaxed and Stephen realized he was going to land just fine, like he had done thousands of times before.

The main gear touched down with the aft set of wheels, followed by a gentle lowering of the forward set. Puffs of smoke emanated from the mains at the same time as the nose gear slowly lowered to an equally smooth touchdown.

"Grease," Judy said, proud to be landing on Earth.

Stephen grabbed the tiller and deftly steered the great plane to the end of the runway.

"Thales, turn right at the high speed, take delta to foxtrot, then to the NASA hangars."

Mars Life

"Delta, foxtrot and to the hangars, Thales."

"And welcome back, we were all turning blue until you touched down like Bob Hoover, nice job."

"My pleasure, nice to be back on Earth, believe me."

With that the great plane, slightly tarnished and worn, followed a "Follow Me" vehicle to a hangar bedecked with flags and buntage. The hangar doors were open and at least a thousand people were all watching the craft as it slowly taxied to the entrance of the hangar. Checklists were completed and shutdown of each engine was accomplished in sequence. The whole process took what seemed like 30 minutes, but soon the deafening quiet that follows after large transport aircraft shut down, ensued. The big Pratts were spinning down as the air stairs were pushed into position. Several trucks with generators and air conditioners, moved into place, connected their various hoses and cables, and soon even the sound of the auxiliary power unit was gone.

The crowds milled around, waiting to see the lone two crew members appear at the top of the stairs. Eventually, the door to the 747 swung open with an appropriate puff of dust, revealing the two heroes dressed in blue jumpsuits. Even with all of the exercise, Earth's gravity took an immediate effect on the weary astronauts. They both reached out for a rail and had to steady themselves. Support crew were near within seconds to offer help and possibly a place to sit. Of course, the VIPs were lined up and after so much time in the mission the crew members were reluctant to give speeches and socialize. But protocol is protocol and part of the duty of an astronaut is to be a public relations spokesperson.

Carefully descending the stairs the crew member shook hands with the NASA administrator, President of the United States, First Lady, Senators..... and the list was long. Finally, the family of each crew member was allowed in for a long awaited reunion. At last the cheering and music began to die down, anticipating a few words from the Commander. Stephen, with a little effort, ascended the stairs of the grandstand placed near the spacecraft. Followed by the co-pilot and chief executive officer, he moved to the microphones, surveyed the crowds, then the sun and began.

"Ladies and gentlemen, it is soooo nice to be back on Earth. Just the warmth of the sun brings tears to my eyes. What a wonderful place this is and by the way, so is Mars. No amount of research, analysis, or simulating could possibly equal being on the red planet. It is completely habitable, I was struck by how easy it was to build structures, find water, and make air. It is a testament to the fine scientists and engineers of NASA and its subcontractors Without your amazing preparation, dedication and confidence a mission of this magnitude would not have been possible. We left two well acclimated pioneers on the planet. Things are going well as we speak. They have food, water, air and a connection to home. Soon others will join them, build communities, have children and form their own unique society. We have much to look forward to, and much support to give these pioneers. Only time will tell how they form their places in the universe.

It was a great journey, both technically and emotionally. We have been through many hardships, many challenges and many changes. And to top it all off, our little run of the mill adventure to another planet was punctuated by the discovery of the alien satellite. Now we have something else to think about. I need to remind everybody that upon discovery of this probe, we made the first move. We were the explorers here and we need to continue to analyze this most profound discovery. These beings are obviously intelligent and I believe, friendly. The information contained in the probe is incredibly important. We must make every effort to study and respond to the information contained in it. As for my crew and I, we humbly accept any opportunity to assist. For now, we would like to spend some much anticipated time with our families. We thank you for your work and support."

Chapter 6: The short wonderful life

"That is a beautiful home they have there, and who's that little fellow?"

Years later, the Spheronts were providing details of their culture, history and technological abilities to their new found friends. Signals monitored and deciphered revealed extraordinary, unexpected description of this race of beings.

Mars Life

First and foremost, the concept of their lifespan being no longer than five earth years was the most important feature. Their first year of life was spent as a baby and child, learning to walk, talk and begin formal schooling. Growth could be observed on a daily basis and clothes were outgrown in weeks.

The most important aspect of Spheront life was initiated at this time. Serious discussions were held by the adults as what the child ultimately would become. The society had to break down achievement into small pieces, that could be managed by in a short time. The leaders' ultimate duty was to provide a schedule for their people, assigning tasks as part of a greater goal. The children's' abilities were considered at the end of this period, and plans made to have them start contributing to their "plan" quickly. Special children were trained to be what they called generators, whose goals were to move the society up a notch in terms of intellectual achievement. Other children were asked to be supporters, whose main goal in life was to create a stabilized culture for the generators to work in. There was in place, a mechanism for the dividing line between these two groups, for movement between the two. The Spheronts believed that a dual society makeup allowed for the most efficient amount of progression. Supporters were encouraged to generate and generators were not looked down upon if they felt more capable of supporting. The line of demarcation was at best theoretical, the important overlying philosophy was growth.

The next phase of their development started at age two, where the Spheronts moved from childhood to adolescence. By this time most goals had been established by the parents and guardians and formal training molded the minds of the young children into the scientists, doctors and teachers of the society. At the end of this period most kids spoke to their friends in pre-career tones, sometimes referring to each other as if they were would in adulthood. Life started to have an air of seriousness at this point.

The young adult phase was next, where every day had meaning. The Spheronts planned their days and broke them into tasks. They still had fun of course but at least three hours a day were devoted to familiarizing themselves with the achievements of the previous "baton" holders. As the larger tasks were broken into smaller increments by the parents and law makers, a plan was followed to achieve a significant goal. For instance, the ability to send a satellite into interstellar space was a goal defined and carried out over many generations. Each generation or baton holder had to design and develop a small piece of the puzzle. Compared to human beings (or Terans), this would equate to about one year of working on a specific project. The

Mars Life

Spheronts understood their ephemeral existence and adjusted their lives to progress as efficiently as possible. The end of the young adult phase included serious considerations as to who their mates would be and where they would ultimately live.

Middle age, or year four began their professional lives, where the tasks anointed to them took up their full attention. Most were married at this point (another duality), started having kids and lived the lives of many professional Terans. The generators worked hard on their assigned tasks, moved as quickly as possible to fulfill or even in some cases extend their creations to help the generation to follow. Any small increment in understanding or operation of a system left by a previous generator would be documented, appreciated and acknowledged. In many cases a generator would be given a piece of hardware (in the case of the satellite builders) that was partially built or designed. The current generator would continue the operation as far as possible to either complete or leave in as mature a position as possible, the system or module. For instance, four generations worked on the communications antenna of the satellite. The first created the mathematics to design this antenna. The second generation evaluated the mathematics and came up with an optimum design. The third generation built the antenna and the forth tested it.

Mars Life

This scenario was repeated on all of the major systems in the satellite, whose total development encompassed at least six generations or roughly 30 years to complete.

Finally, the Spheronts lived out their final year, typically year five, at a slower pace. This year was spent in retirement, where again, every day counted. The Spheront government, which by the way was planet wide, made sure that each retiree was taken care of and appreciated for his or her contributions. They had the advantage of being able to hand off their tasks to the next generation of middle age generators or supporters and watching the growth of the society. They could if they wanted, continue to contribute or critique. They could alternatively, observe and relax.

The story of the Spheronts reached most earth dwellers and made quite a few of them consider their place in this world (so to speak). Spheronts made the best of their limited time alive, made long terms plans, ambitious plans, that took multiple generations to accomplish. They were able to conquer space in this way and create many other major achievements. Earth dwellers had to consider this and ask what they could achieve in such a long lived society as they were privileged to experience.

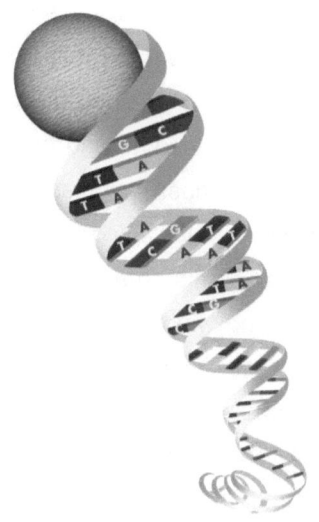

Chapter 7:   The Hybrid Society

"There they are, wave...man, they look great"

As earth learned more and more about the lives and aspirations of the Spheronts, earthbound scientists were able through the data stream to determine the genetic structure of the species (as it had been codified and transmitted as a file). They found that the DNA was in fact very similar to humans. This of course, started a round of discussions about the religious significance vs. the evolutionists (again). During the debates that were carried out in offices, taverns and homes, the scientists went about their business in objectively asking several important questions. Including, what would happen if Terans and Spheronts mated? What would the offspring, assuming viability, look like? A particular group, located at Johns Hopkins Medical Center developed a simulator in software that could in fact predict viability and morphology. Along with the predictions came probabilities. These probabilities showed how accurate or confidant this simulator considered its calculations. The morphologies were broken down into groups centered around certain gene combinations. For instance if genes that developed ears were combined between species, what would the new ears look like? The medical researchers tried 100s of different gene combinations and found to their surprise, that the two species were indeed compatible. As expected the morphologies were the melding of certain traits and followed the general rules of genetics. At some point in time, the realization was made that mating could in fact be safe, although it was determined that a "test tube baby" approach would be the best initial move.

271

But now what? Try it?

As the debate about the finding continued, one of the researchers simulated the lifespan of the offspring from the combination of the human and Spheront. They were able to determine that the child would have a significantly longer life span and grow up more at a human rate of change. In essence, it was found that there would be a compromise in growth speed and the length of life.

In addition to the change in life span, it was discovered that mentally, the offspring would be significantly advanced. Several portions of the new brain would have many more neurons, the physical size in fact would be slightly larger. Areas of the brain normally associated with logic and artistic expressions were very advanced and revealed to the researchers that the new offspring could be a major step ahead for both species.

The next question of course was how much could the new species achieve? This question was followed closely by "how would feel about their less capable parents?"

Again, the discussions went on, sometimes in public venues, sometimes on news broadcasts, but always with a sense of urgency. This was certainly news that could not be suppressed for long. The Spheronts would also have some interesting opinions about this discovery.

Chapter 8:   The NASA debates

"Welcome to Mars, welcome to our home, come on in and have something to eat"

The most urgent and comprehensive discussions came at the NASA venues.   Scientists, social scientists, philosophers and other professionals gathered at Cape Canaveral to discuss the short, medium and long term impacts on the potential hybrid being.

Clearly, the decision to share the discovery with the Spheronts was necessary.   Assuming they could detect and de modulate signals sent from earth, a program was initiated to use the 1000 foot antenna at Arecibo, Puerto Rico to start a line of communications with the Spheront world, optimizing the bandwidth and thus, information flow. At first, signals were sent in a very simple fashion, in such a way as to allow the recipients the ability to decode the messages. Carl Sagan's images on board the Voyager series spacecraft were sent many times, followed by adaptations to these images to develop a common language based on the "hieroglyphics" of the original message. The timing of the transmissions was precisely controlled with long wait periods to allow the Spheronts, assuming they were listening, to consider what they had received.

They did in fact respond, and told their story as well as translated their languages to the awaiting scientists at NASA. After significantly more debate between the world's scientists and the world's governments, the decision ended up in the hands of the secretary general of the United Nations. Only he could speak for all countries on earth.

He listened to the scientists, the politicians and most importantly, the people, who in general were anxious to meet the new species. There were so many questions to be answered, about life there, religion, their politics, economy, etc. The curiosity was intense and was the basis for a speech made the appointed world's spokesman.

Mars Life

A natural leader for all people on earth was the secretary general of the United Nations. At the time, her name was Jocylin O'Hara from Ireland. She had a background in philosophy and science from the University of Cambridge, had grown up in an ambassador's home. A unifying spirit, she identified with the intellects of the day as well as had an appreciation for the efforts and abilities of the more common peoples. She believed that the efforts of a street sweeper had importance in this world and provided a function necessary to allow all mankind to progress. As a consequence of her intellect and sociological "compass", she was the perfect person to speak for all earthlings. It was a first time that the United Nations spoke for us all, as apposed to being the referee to conflicts as history has imposed on them.

Jocylin thought carefully about her speech, consulted her mentors and read the NASA communication reports with the Spheronts. The fact that this was the first speech that represented all mankind did not escape her attention. She thought about our history, our present state of affairs, about how different cultures would respond and most importantly, how we should make our first interstellar expression.

She found it appropriate to talk about one of the most important allegories in our history, that of Plato's discussion of how two equal but different genders of our species came to pass. It expressed an insight that was important for the Spheronts to understand. Our first expression was founded on reason and based on the recognition of our differences with the Spheronts as well as our similarities.

She mounted the stage of the main Hall of the United Nations in New York City, waited for the noise to die down and proceeded with the following speech:

"This is a story is about the creation of the sexes on our planet. It has deep meaning to us Terans and is representative of how we have adjusted to difference and adapted to new circumstance. According to legend, a very long time ago there was man, woman and a combination of both on our earth. The combination had four hands, four feet, two faces and had both male and female organs. This combination person was very powerful, gaining the strengths of both genders. This worried the Gods, who were most powerful and looked over us, especially Zeus (the most powerful of Gods), as the combination person had started to defy the Gods themselves. Zeus decided to cut the combination person in two, making a single woman and single man, who to this day remain in search of each other. The art in the period of this story always portrayed men and women in profile as a testament to the strength of the peoples' belief. This is a natural way of life as explained by an allegory written by Plato, one of our wisest philosophers. In similar fashion as the two halves seeking each other, so to should the two halves of interstellar beings seek each other. Because it is natural. And so too should we extend our help and knowledge to these new friends. I suggest we send viable DNA to these people in an effort to extend their lifetimes. Think of what they could produce in a lifespan of one hundred years as apposed to their normal five! Our cell genome projects have yielded significant new discoveries that can help both of our species. Their's is so close to ours that we can identify the special aging gene and give them instructions as to how to modify it to extend their lives.

It is important to learn however, how much they have achieved by teamwork and planning. This life style will be their gift to us, as we could achieve so much more by following their example.

Establish a link and tell them of our plan. Lets increase the our communication abilities with dedicated radio astronomy antennas and start the dialog. This will benefit the Spheronts and all mankind."

Mars Life

And so it was, the comm links were established, knowledge traded and the modified DNA was developed to make the long trip. It was placed in stasis and sent along with many other important gifts to the Spheronts. The satellite was designed around the latest propulsion technology using ion and Biefield/Brown effect rockets. Although it took many years for it to make its journey, the wait for a return package was much shorter as the Spheronts had dedicated several generations of engineers to the emergency design and development of an earth bound probe with advanced propulsion technology. In the future there became hope of establishing a base or bases between the two worlds where we could meet the Spheronts themselves.

Epilogue: The Next Mission

The new crew had just landed in a gleaming new replacement for the Thales which was now hung in a new Hall of Space Exploration in the Smithsonian. There were twenty people on board this time, some were planning to stay (with mission control's consent this time). Benjamin, Nanci and their son, Quinton, were waiting for them and watched their approach and landing. Life had been hard but the ease of making shelters and finding plenty of water *made it tolerable. Benjamin had constructed five new buildings, two new water storage facilities and a pool inside one of the greenhouses. They had learned how to heat the greenhouses and other buildings with passive solar innovations and the propellant factory's residual heat. One of the buildings was three stories tall and received enough radiant energy from the sun to heat itself nicely. The original cave had been turned into a storage area after some modifications. Most importantly, food was now in abundance, most of the seeds had germinated, grown and multiplied. In fact, the air inside the structures was mountain pure and had turned into a more pleasant fragrant smelling mixture of oxygen and nitrogen combined with the scents from the plants. There came times where the plants produced so much oxygen that the colonists had to vent it outside. With the new arrivals, they would join in the making of several more structures, including more greenhouses. The little colony would slowly grow in the next several years into a small village, with hundreds of people living there in all stratas of life. The new crew also brought a present for the original colonists, who had grown to three individuals..... a puppy.*

Mars Life

As for the Spheronts, several way stations had been constructed between the Earth and the Spheront home world which allowed travel between the planets to be a bit easier. The two species transferred members back and forth, cross pollinating science and culture. For the Terans, a new sense of oneness evolved. The Terans had started to realize that they were in fact more like each other that ever before. The wars and skirmishes based on political and personal motivations slowly started to been seen as idiocy. People started to really help each other and as a result, much needless suffering and bloodshed was eliminated. It was the perfect formula for peace.

The Spheronts lived longer, prospered from their friendship with the Terans and in turn transferred their great knowledge and work ethic to the Terans.

The two species together were stronger as a result of their bond and in time considered looking even farther into space for other life forms.

About the Author

Kevin Shoemaker was born in New York City in April of 1954. A son of an actress and musician turned professor. He has lived in several states and has been educated in the fields of philosophy, radio astronomy and antenna design. He has authored several technical papers and has nine patents in the fields of aviation, antenna design and meteorology. In addition, he is an avid pilot and boat owner and holds several certificates for operating aircraft, helicopters and performing flight instruction. Currently he works as a consultant to a satellite manufacturing firm, designing antennas for spacecraft. Mr. Shoemaker is a father of one daughter and one son and lives near Boulder, Colorado with his wife, Judi.

www.ingramcontent.com/pod-product-compliance
Lightning Source LLC
Chambersburg PA
CBHW021958010726
47494CB00003B/793